SAVED BY GRACE

BROTHERS OF BELLE FOURCHE: BOOK 4

KARI TRUMBO

Saved by Grace

Copyright © 2019 Kari Trumbo

All rights reserved.

ISBN-13: 978 1798135792

All rights reserved under International and Pan-American Copyright Conventions

This is a work of fiction. Names, characters, places, and incidents are either the products of the author's imagination or are used fictitiously, and any resemblance to actual persons, living or dead, business establishments, events, or locales is purely coincidental.

No part of this book may be reproduced or transmitted in any form or by any electronic or mechanical means, including photocopying, recording or by any information storage and retrieval system, without the written permission of the publisher, except where permitted by law.

Where used, the KJV version of the Bible is quoted.

Cover Design by Carpe Librum Book Design

For thou has possessed my reins: thou hast covered me in my mother's womb. I will praise thee; for I am fearfully and wonderfully made: marvelous are they works; and that my soul knoweth right well.
Psalm 139: 13-14

CHAPTER 1

Belle Fourche, South Dakota
August, 1900

He'd seen her kind before. Cody Hammond balanced on his stool, his one leg braced against the desk. It was an allowance the bank made based on his condition. The petite woman hesitated at the large front doors, her look wary. She wasn't local, didn't know immediately where to go. Her brow furrowed deeply as she searched for a friendly face. Her gaze landed on him briefly, flitted along, then swung back and she gave just a hint of a smile. He leaned farther over his counter, ducking his head to hide his eyes and appear busy, glad of the bars that blocked him from getting too close to anyone.

"Excuse me?" A soft voice with a hint of an accent spoke just over his head. "I need your help."

If he'd been standing, he would've towered over her. But that would never happen. Instead, she would look down at him, as she was doing now, because he was stuck working from a chair. He sighed and laid down his pen then gave her his attention. Chivalry had been ingrained in him, both from his father and from the English Army, and he couldn't just ignore her plea. "Yes, miss?" For she did look like a young miss with hair like flax in two braids down the sides of her head and a purple dress about the color of lilacs.

"I," she paused and glanced quickly at the other two men down the counter, then lowered her voice, "didn't know where to ask and we couldn't find the post office. Can you tell me where to find the Oleson place? It's rather urgent. I'm lost without your help." Her wide green-gold eyes searched him and he squared his shoulders, preparing to send her on her way. Most people didn't feel comfortable right off talking to him, as if his infirmity was somehow contagious. That she would even speak to him when two other men stood at identical stations was a mystery, and he hated mysteries.

He pursed his lips and held back from saying what his bitter, vicious thoughts wanted him to.

Rules. Manners. The voice as old as time scolded him.

"You keep on driving, right out of town. Almost an hour by wagon, shorter on horseback." He pointed in the general direction she should go, even from inside the walls of the bank, she would be able to find it. There were only two ways in and out of town.

Women were shifty, untrustworthy, meddlesome and conniving. He could say all those things in his head, but not at the bank or anywhere else, and especially not to their faces. It was a battle he'd had with himself many times—bark the way he wanted to, or hold his tongue and act the way he'd been raised.

Her lip turned up just slightly and she curtsied,

making him shift uncomfortably on his stool. There was no room for such cultured actions in Belle Fourche.

"Thank you kindly," she retreated a few steps, still staring at him. Then, with a swift turn, she hurried from the bank as if she were late to a party.

Unmarried women of suitable age were a rarity in Belle Fourche. Men were a dime a dozen. They came from near and far to be part of the cattle trade, but women were married off quick as you please. Cody Hammond had only been in Belle Fourche a few months and he'd already been to a few weddings, including that of his sister, Anne. She'd married Eli Oleson of the very ranch that woman was headed to. He scratched his chin and plucked his watch from his vest pocket. He still had an hour to work and had no way of getting out to the ranch anyway, to see what trouble this woman would stir up. Yet, his curiosity nagged. He lived in town, because there were no jobs for him out at the Broken Circle O. He hadn't even let them try to find one. So there would be no way to figure out what was so urgent until Anne came to visit him.

"Hammond!" The banker called to Cody from his office in the back corner.

He slid his crutch under his left arm and made his way to the office. Despite how little he spoke with the other men who worked in the bank, the banker, Mr. Harvey Langerford, seemed to appreciate him. It made working there bearable.

"Hammond, I've been over this stack of numbers five times and I can't come up with the same number twice." He slid a long column of figures to the other side of his desk. From the moment he'd realized Cody could do huge sums in his head, Mr. Langerford had tried to stump him. He'd most likely done the whole thing five times just to make sure of his answer before he called Cody in.

It took him a minute to look down the column and do the figures. He waited a few extra moments, just to make the banker feel better. "Seven thousand nine-hundred and ten dollars, and twenty-nine cents." He sat in the chair with as much grace as possible and leaned his crutch against his boss's desk. He rubbed the sore area just above where his knee should've been. He sometimes could feel pain in parts of his missing limb and there was no way to relieve the ache.

"Was that all you called me in for, parlor tricks?" He often felt like a parlor dog when Langerford brought him in for a test. It was as if he'd been taught to do his little stunt so he would be kept around a little longer.

"Yes, and no." The older man smiled as he leaned forward in his chair. "I think you hold a lot of promise in that head. But until you start making people want to borrow money from you, I can't raise you from the position you're in. You know I look for the best in people. It's what brings people into my bank, and I need that in the person who will join me."

They'd had the conversation before. It may have been Langerford's personality, or it could have just been that he was the only bank in town. Either way, Cody had no interest in becoming a simpering ninny. Langerford was sure if Cody could manage to just look somber, not so angry, he could have a different job. Behind a desk, not bars. It would mean more money and he could live more easily. Part of him wanted it, another was too afraid to dream. He didn't belong in an office, he wasn't even sure he belonged at the bank.

"Yes, I know. Stop growling at the patrons. I'll keep working on it." But he wouldn't. He'd been *this* man for so long, the man who refused the help of others because when people cared, they had the power to change him. Change was difficult, except at the hands of someone who claimed to love, like Anne, his sister. She'd forced him to get better once, long ago. But she wouldn't again.

At least he was better than he'd been in the asylum, where they'd strapped him into his wheelchair with thick leather fastenings because he hated being there so much he'd tried to escape on many occasions. They had tired of him, but not as much as he'd tired of living there.

Mr. Langerford laughed and pressed his palms to the top of the desk as he stood. "I know you'll try. Underneath that grim exterior is a good man. If you watch me, keep learning, there's no reason we can't be partners here someday. Just think of it. You could control all of this." He waived his hand slowly over the whole room.

Cody pulled on his high neck shirt and refused to take the bait. He was never sure how to act when someone did or said something that could be seen as kind. Cody was usually so curt with people, it didn't happen often, and if history was any indicator it meant he'd be dealt a bad turn soon. He wasn't even all that kind to his sister Anne, as it was partly her fault he'd been put in the asylum to begin with. Her needs had forced him to live through things, see things, no man should have to. Though he loved her, he couldn't excuse her and he couldn't accept kindness from her or anyone else.

"I don't see that ever happening, sir. Thank you, anyway." He gripped the crutch and slid it under his arm.

"Please, Hammond. I don't know anyone else in town I'd rather work with. At least think about it. It could come with some benefits that will be arriving shortly."

He turned and kept his pace for the door. Knowing that Langerford was pleading with him made his stomach clench. He'd already looked at every possible outcome in working for the bank and none of them led to his own office. There just wasn't any possibility he could change enough to make it happen. He ignored the man's words and headed for the door.

Perhaps Anne would visit the following night and let him in on the excitement at the ranch. More likely, she wouldn't see him until the Sunday service she insisted he come to, more so that she wouldn't have to visit than that she truly cared about his soul. Though she need not worry, that particular organ had been dead for a long time.

CHAPTER 2

Father's old leather gloves didn't fit well and made a strange creaking sound when she bent her fingers, but she still had to drive the wagon. No one else would and they had to keep moving forward. Natalie Oleson's brothers rode far back behind them, taking their time as always, leaving her to deal with both the driving and worrying about Father.

Her father caught her glancing behind the wagon and laid his hand softly on her arm. "Don't mind them, girl. Just keep your eyes on where we're going. I see familiar posts up ahead." His old gnarled hands shifted to grip the seat on either side of him. Though he'd normally kept his head bent against the sun, now it was up, tilted to see the horizon ahead.

It would be much easier to mind the road before her if she didn't have to constantly think about her brothers, her past, her sick father, and their destination…their future. Though there did seem to be poles ahead with a large arched sign between them, like the ones her father had told her about. The man with the dark hair and striking gray eyes at the bank hadn't given her any marks to look for. It *had* been about an hour, that was the only clue that the sign ahead might, indeed, finally be their destination.

Her father coughed and wheezed next to her and his breathing came in ragged contractions, but the closer they got the more he calmed. "This is it, Natalie. I haven't been to this ranch in decades, but this is it. Nathan and his wife will make sure you all have a place to stay, work to do, and food in your bellies." He leaned back against the wooden box of the wagon, letting his shoulders relax as he closed his eyes in the sun. That wooden box had been his workshop and their shelter for as long as she could remember. "I'm sure it's where I'll spend the rest of my days, few as they might be."

Her heart constricted at the thought. They'd already lost Mama, almost ten years before. Though nothing was ever a surprise to the Lord, losing her father so soon would surely be wrong. The Lord was a holy and just God, He wouldn't do such a thing to her. "Don't say things like that Papa, you'll be just fine. We'll have a nice visit and head right on into the mountains you always told us about. Wouldn't it be grand to see them together?" She had to divert his thoughts. He couldn't think about dying, it's all he'd been worried about for the past few months. She'd been tasked with getting them to South Dakota, then to Belle Fourche, and finally to the Broken Circle O, so that her father felt comfortable enough to die. Now she wished the grueling trip had taken even longer. She wasn't ready to let him go.

He hung his head, then patted her knee. "My girl, the Black Hills are even better than I told you, but there's a reason I never brought you here to see them. My brother and I haven't been in the same state for thirty years. Belle Fourche wasn't even a town when I left, South Dakota was only a territory, a rough place. I came here to break timber and help Nathan build the ranch he'd envisioned, but never planned to stay. South Dakota just wasn't big enough for two Olesons. When he realized I was fixing to leave him, he was furious and I've never felt right about coming back since."

She knew the story, but her father had earned the respect of a listening ear, so she would always oblige. Since Mama's death, she'd always tried to do just as her papa told her so he wouldn't have to get angry or worry. She'd try to become Mama for her brothers. Letting go was so hard. "I know, Papa. I just hope all can be forgiven after so long. We probably have family we've never met waiting for us." Her hands trembled, more from worry about meeting her uncle than from fatigue. She'd driven that wagon for the last six months as her father's health had declined. Would her uncle take them in or turn them out? Would the family she didn't know care enough about her wayward brothers to help? She was stuck between wanting to stop the wagon and hold onto the last few moments of life as she'd always known it, having Papa all to herself, and relinquishing the aching burden of being the head of the family, since her brothers didn't want the job.

They passed acres upon acres of pastures so huge she couldn't see cattle, nor the other row of fence marking the back edge. A huge white house waited for them, with various out buildings and a few scattered, distant cabins. If those belonged to Nathan's children, he may not have room for them. If they were workers, they might be able to save him some wages. If her unruly brothers would actually work.

Natalie pulled the wagon to a stop in front of the

house and held her breath as an older woman came out, shielding her eyes from the sun. She stared at Kevin, Natalie's father, for a few moments, then her mouth dropped open and she hollered back to the house behind her, "Nathan, come on out here. I think you'll want to." She hurried down the stairs, her boots clicking on the wood, and she reached up for Papa's hand. "Kevin, I never thought I'd live to see the day," she whispered. Her gaze flicked to Natalie. "And who's this?"

Natalie didn't want to be rude but talking made Papa's fits of coughing worse. She peeled off her stiff leather glove and thrust out her hand, glad to be rid of it. "I'm your niece, ma'am, Natalie Oleson."

She laughed, "Natalie." Her eyes glistened as she shot a glance to Papa and smiled. "I knew you hadn't given up on Nathan." She gave Natalie's hand a good shake. "You can call me Aunt Maretta."

Just then, a man who looked much like her father stepped out of the house and onto the porch, except, unlike her father, he was as hearty as a bowl of stew. It was like seeing a younger version of her own father, though Nathan was the older of the two.

"Kevin?" He seemed as mystified as his wife.

Her father nodded, but his strength was waning. He already slumped in his seat and she gripped his arm to keep him from sliding down farther. One more fit of coughing and he wouldn't be able to hold himself up.

"Papa is very sick. Can we move him inside? I'll wait out here for my brothers."

The woman's smile grew even larger. "Brothers?"

She said a little prayer that they would be welcome, and not only that, she prayed they would mind themselves. "Yes, three of them. They should be along shortly.

They lagged behind on the ride out. They're a bit of a handful."

Aunt Maretta's eyes twinkled as she let Uncle Nathan help her father down. "I know just what to do with boys. We raised four of our own."

A little bit of the burden she'd carried in reprimanding and helping raise three now fully grown but unruly boys slipped from her shoulders. "Thank you, ma'am. They need all the help they can get."

CHAPTER 3

Dust rose from the wide street as booted feet and horse hooves tramped the earth outside the bank and Cody took a moment to lean against the front to fix his tie. Though the hat of choice in Belle Fourche was a floppy sort, favored by cowboys, he preferred a bowler. He'd purchased the one he had on before he'd left London, though people generally stared when he wore it. It did little to keep sun from his face, but reminded him of England itself, the culture and clothing, which was the only warmth he'd been able to muster for years.

When he'd first come to Belle Fourche, following his sister Anne, he'd told her he thought family was the most important thing. He'd made her believe he'd come because she meant something, and she had, she'd been his plan of escape. He'd needed her to believe family was important so that she would help him. Instead, she'd found him a job and he was surviving on his own, which was exactly how he truly wanted to be. Alone.

He did a quick search of the street for the woman in

lavender while he rested. Though he usually paid little heed to women, this one was curious. She'd come to him, when there had been many other choices, even after he'd given her his usual glower. People didn't do unexpected things. He understood people and how they acted and responded. But she'd done just the opposite. He wanted to sit and make a list as he usually did when faced with a confusing situation, but there wasn't time. Lists took away his worry, and compiling one of all her potential responses to him would go a long way to ease his mind.

The woman had been in a hurry an hour before, but he'd hoped she'd had to visit the market or run other errands before pulling out of town, allowing him to slake his curiosity about her arrival in Belle Fourche. It was rare that he knew of someone's appearance in town before anyone else. After a few minutes of searching, he could find no one who looked remotely like her and he pushed away from the wall, sliding his crutch under his arm.

The boarding house where he lived was only a few blocks away and he slowly took his usual route with purpose along the wood walk, others dodging out of his way. It was the same group of people he saw almost every day, since he didn't walk near the market or livery to get home where the people who visited were different every day.

Those who came to town to shop only visited the bank briefly, rarely dawdling. The bustling side of town was blocks away, by the shops and the doctor. At the thought of Dr. Spight, his gaze wandered down the street. His sister wouldn't know they had visitors out at the ranch yet, but he could go and see if they had been expecting anyone. She might know of an impending arrival, especially an urgent one as the woman had said.

He made his way down the street, exhausted by the time he reached the little house that passed as a clinic. He glanced quickly in both directions before crossing, then maneuvered himself up the boardwalk steps to the doctor's office. It was a house that had been converted into a clinic and painted a dark mulberry with white trim and shutters to stand out from the rest of the buildings on the street. It looked like a two-story home smashed between two false-front stores. He glanced in the large front window and didn't see anyone waiting in the seats to be seen, so he pushed the door open.

His sister, Anne, sat at a large desk in the front with her head bent over some papers and a thick roll of white gauze at her side. She stared down at a large accounting book, drumming her long fingers.

"Anne." Though he'd tried on occasion to keep his actual feelings for her under his hat, most of the time it didn't matter. She knew he wasn't a kind man and that he had little care for her anymore. He couldn't afford to. He'd loved her once and it had cost him dearly, then he'd tried to love her again and she'd turned him away.

She glanced up and pursed her lips. "Cody, good afternoon. What brings you by?"

Though she didn't offer a seat, he sat in the hard, wooden chair facing the desk and rested his crutch against it. "Isn't a man allowed to see how his sister is getting along? Especially after she married a man she'd only known for a brief time. I worry." He didn't really. Eli was responsible enough and had proven Cody needn't worry about Anne at all. In fact, with Eli there, *he* didn't really need to stay in Belle Fourche at all, except he had nowhere else to go but back to England, which was his plan as soon as he'd saved away enough for the trip and living expenses once he got there.

"If you actually had any worry about me what-so-ever, then you could stop by and I would invite you to sit to tea, however," She tipped her head back to her paper and let her accusation hang in the air like the stench of skunk baking in the sun.

He finally removed his hat and set it in his lap, but Anne didn't glance up at him again. He'd wanted her to come with him, to return home to England and start over. He'd begged her to forget America and Eli. Before he'd been put away, he'd had a great desire to do right by England, and had convinced Anne she needed to do the same. However, in the years while they had been separated, Anne came to America and had fallen in love. She now had a great desire to stay with Eli, so he'd temporarily given up. He'd cultivated the distrust between them with his return and it would be difficult to pry information from her.

"You have a guest."

She glanced at the door, then at him, tilting her head slightly. "I see no one."

He laughed, and it was a rare enough occurrence that even Anne's forehead wrinkled in confusion. "I mean, out at the ranch. Someone came into the bank today, looking for the Broken Circle O."

Anne finally set down her pencil and sat up straight in her seat. "A visitor? I wonder who it could be?"

Drat, he'd hoped she'd had some clue. The lavender woman was a mystery and he needed more facts for the lists he would compose later, trying to figure her out. "The Olesons didn't tell you of expected guests?" He worked hard to keep his voice level. No need to make Anne wonder about his curiosity.

"No, I'm afraid not. Once Eli and I wed, there was no reason for me to spend much time at the house. We have our own. I don't often know who Nathan and Maretta entertain unless Eli has a mind to tell me."

Though he wanted to know more, her story made sense. She would want to enjoy even the little scrap of a house Eli had provided. Even Eli's small cabin was better than what she'd been living in before. He shuddered to himself. The little shed she'd lived in behind the clinic was almost the exact size of the one he'd burned to the ground to get away from the asylum. Visiting her there had been a trial and he'd been happy to see her move her few things out of it.

"Was that your only reason for coming in, to let me know that you knew of guests at the Olesons' before I did?" Her top lip stiffened.

He hadn't meant to offend her, never *really* meant to. It always just seemed to happen. He simply harbored so much animosity about what happened that sometimes it came out without his permission. "No, I stopped in to see if you might know who it was. I didn't recognize her."

"Her?" Anne's eyebrows rose and her gray eyes, the only thing that was strikingly similar between the two siblings, widened. "I assumed you meant a man, a cowboy, someone looking for work."

He chuckled at the thought of Miss Lavender Gingham as a cowboy. "No, not unless you're hiring women of marrying age for your hands, but that doesn't seem like something Nathan would do."

"Surely not," Anne huffed as she stood. "I think I'll be closing up a little early. Thank you for stopping in. Will I be seeing you on Sunday?" She efficiently cleaned and cleared the desk as she spoke.

He hated begging for a ride, because it meant they would have to drive him all the way back in, but he was itching to know more. "You know nothing about this? Not a jot?"

Anne slipped off her nurse's cap and left it on a shelf, replacing it with a black hat she pinned in place. "As I said, I know as much as you do. By your refusal to answer, I would assume you don't want to go. I'll see you there anyway." She kissed his cheek as she went for her riding coat by the door. "Pull the door closed on your way out."

She'd always been a little bossy, and now he'd have to go to church to find out about the visitors. He generally hated get-togethers but the Olesons often offered to bring him out to supper at the ranch after service. He always refused, because he detested church anyway and extending it beyond its time would be torturous, but if they offered this Sunday he might just accept. It would be a surreptitious way to learn what the connection was between the Olesons and Miss Lavender.

CHAPTER 4

Aunt Maretta put Papa in a room with a large bed and window that let in sunlight through the day. Though Natalie wanted to get to know her aunt, her newfound cousins, and the ranch, she still had to care for him. He was too sick for her to leave. After the first full day of rest, he opened his eyes.

"My girl." He smiled and reached for her hand. It was chilly to the touch, shocking in the warm room.

"I'm here." She squeezed his hand back and noticed for the first time how boney it was. Her father had been strong and capable his whole life, had been up until about six months before. Something had happened to bring him down, but not quickly like a cold. This had been a slow, steady illness that had robbed him of his strength.

"I want you to promise me you and your brothers will not continue this business. It's too hard, takes you too far away. I spent too much of my life driving the cart around, whittling, worrying, making plans for better models. You don't need that. Let the men who have companies do it."

She couldn't let it go. It was her only means to provide for herself and her brothers. "What else do we know?" She'd never considered that her years of watching her father bring help to those who needed it would go to waste. She'd tried so hard to impress him all these years with her ability to learn, to be the son who paid attention and wanted to help. He couldn't make her let that go.

"You can finally learn how to be a wife and mother from your aunt, instead of a working man's daughter. Meet some people through your cousins. They are about your age. Meet a man and grow old with him."

She chuckled for his benefit, but her insides quaked at the idea. She had no such wish. She'd never felt comfortable around anyone but her family. The only exception were the invalids who would come and be fitted for wooden legs by her father. Those only stayed around for a few days. A husband was for a lifetime.

"Unless your husband is in the business of making arms and legs, and stays put to do it, don't ever do this job again." He closed his eyes and breathed deeply. It rattled deep in his chest and he wheezed, "Where are the boys?"

The *boys*, as her father had always called them, had avoided the house since their arrival midday the day before. "They are in the bunkhouse, giving Barton a hard time about being their age and strapped to a woman already."

Father laughed for a moment then stopped. "They didn't get to see the good things, or chose to forget them. Life was good with your mother. I hope Nathan and Maretta can show them what I couldn't."

They would have to grow up soon. Aunt Maretta had told them she would give them time to work out their anger, then she would put them to work on the farm. None of them had been particularly pleased about the prospect. They were still holed up in the bunkhouse because Barton let it slip that his ma never went in there.

"I hope Aunt Maretta and Uncle Nathan can beat some sense into them. They are plain spoiled." She bit her tongue at the hurt in her father's eyes. He was the one who should've whipped them, but never had.

"If they need a whippin', Nathan will do it. He isn't opposed to the switch."

She remembered clearly the one and only time she'd talked back to her father. They'd been on a long drive somewhere in the South and she'd been hot and tired. She'd learned that day that discomfort was no excuse to be rude. Her backside had hurt for days, reminding her to be mindful of her parents. Her brothers had been too hard-headed to let the switch bother them when they were young, then Mama got sick and Papa was too busy caring for her and trying to work. The boys were allowed to run free, especially after she died.

"They are a little old for hickory," she said, trying to sound as if she had any control over them at all. If she had managed to keep watch over her brothers, for Mama, maybe losing her wouldn't still hurt so badly.

"Maybe, maybe not. If I'd been in a mind to be a parent when they were still boys, they might not need it now."

Natalie pushed away from the bed and grabbed the cloth hanging from the wash basin. She wet it and gently washed her father's face. "Don't concern yourself with them just now. Rest. You're already looking better and it's only been one day." She forced herself to smile, though she didn't feel it.

"I do feel a little stronger," her father said. "Send Nathan up when you go downstairs. Go, get to know your aunt a bit."

It was the last thing she wanted to do. So far, she'd only allowed herself to leave her father's side to use the privy and get food. "I'd rather just stay with you."

He patted her hand and the chill of it frightened her. He wasn't warming up the longer he was awake as she'd expected him to.

"Go. I won't die while you're gone and I need to speak to my brother."

She couldn't ignore a direct order, no matter how much she hated to do it. "All right. I'll get him and let him know you'd like to see him." She bit her lip for a moment. Though her father had always welcomed her thoughts, they had never expressed love verbally and her heart raced with worry that it would bother him to hear it, but the words had to be said, before it was too late. "I love you, Papa."

He chuckled softly and shooed her from her seat. "I know, now go on."

Natalie did her best to remember how to get out of the house that seemed to wind around itself in the upper floors, with little nooks and hidden rooms. She'd gotten lost on her way out in the evening the night before. Leaning against the banister of a staircase, she paused to listen and the sound of voices below drew her. After getting turned around once, she made her way to the main floor where Aunt Maretta was in the kitchen with a blonde woman who had the curliest hair Natalie had ever seen. She held a child on each hip.

"Natalie! You made it down, you must be starving. I

don't think I've seen you take a bite since you arrived. This is your cousin by law, Lula, and her babies, Connie and Peter. She's Barton's wife and spends much of her time here with me." Aunt Maretta didn't seem to breathe as she bustled about the kitchen.

Natalie gave a slight curtsey, since Lula's hands were busy. "It's nice to meet you."

Lula nodded in return. "You'll soon find you've got more sisterly company than you'll know what to do with. Arnold is married to Stephenia, she's the teacher at the Belle Fourche school but is home for the summer now, Eli is married to Anne who is a nurse, and Conrad is married to my closest friend Izzy. Though, most people call her Isabelle now."

She hadn't thought about Maretta's four boys as married men, but they would be the same ages as her brothers and definitely marrying age. "So, all four of your boys are married, then."

Aunt Maretta spoke while she fixed a plate of food. "Yes, some earlier than we expected, some later, but all are happy."

She hadn't been happy in a long time. She'd lived, following her father from town to town, struggling to get a handle on her brothers and make them continue to follow. But happiness had been just out of reach for years. "I can't wait to meet them all."

Lula turned to her and smiled. "The time to do that will be Sunday, after the church service. The family meal after church is the one thing no Oleson can avoid."

Except her family was full of Olesons who'd never been to a family meal. "I look forward to it."

Maretta set the plate of food at the table and waved her over to it. "Sit now, child, and eat. We'll get both you and your father feeling better before you know it."

"He would like to see Uncle Nathan, if possible." Natalie glanced over the plate of sliced chicken with day-old baked potato and carrots. It was more food on one plate than she'd ever seen before.

"I'll send him up in just a bit. You ran off upstairs so quickly yesterday, I don't think I even got the chance to welcome you. The Broken Circle O is here for any Oleson, anytime. I hope you'll stay a good long while."

Natalie set her fork back down next to her plate, her hunger pangs vanished. If her father was right, she may never leave.

CHAPTER 5

Preacher O'Hare generally didn't interest Cody all that much anyway, but giving the man his attention was even harder when he just wanted that part of the day to end. Cody sat next to Anne on the very end of the pew, her husband's family filling the whole row all the way to the center and beyond. There were so many people with the Oleson family that day, they'd had to spread out, forcing other families to move. He'd have gladly given up his seat, but there would be no peace from his sister if he didn't attend.

The whole church had been angling to hear about the four new Olesons in attendance, and he'd held back from the group and their pecking, not wanting to be around so many people. But now that the service had started, he couldn't help leaning forward to catch a glimpse of the woman with the brown hair who'd come to the bank. Her brothers sat next to her and though she didn't look anything like her siblings, *they* could've easily been brothers with Conrad, Arnold, Eli, and Barton instead of cousins. They all had the same hard, squared jaw, the same thin lips and long noses, the same cowboy attire.

One young cowhand glanced over his shoulder and smiled at the woman Cody had come to think of as Miss Lavender and the brother closest to her flicked the boy's ear loud enough for the *thwack* to carry through the church. Miss Lavender's eyes widened and she gripped her brother's hand as chuckles rose from various places through the church. Her cheeks were thin, but seemed to plump up a bit with a blush. He couldn't remember the last time he'd witnessed a woman do that.

When the service ended, the Olesons waited around until everyone got to speak to the newcomers. From what Cody could hear, it sounded like the family was there to stay. What he couldn't figure out was why they had been in such an urgent rush to get to the ranch. No one seemed to be able to answer that. Of course, no one else knew they had been in a rush besides Cody.

After the service, her light green eyes caught sight of him from where she spoke to Lula at the end of the pew and she slowly angled her way toward him. When she reached him, she sat and a slight scent of soap and talc lingered around her. Even though she wore a different color that day, her name had almost been branded as Miss Lavender in his thoughts. She gave him a soft smile and he wasn't sure if he should—or even if he could—return it or not.

"I'm Natalie Oleson, and I never thanked you properly for your help earlier this week. It was kind of you to give me directions."

Kindness wasn't something he was often accused of and he hadn't really given her anything except the minimum that was required. "I did no more than anyone else would've."

She nodded, but her gaze caught and held on his leg, just above his left knee, or what should've been a knee. Every time he met someone, he always hoped they wouldn't stare, wouldn't notice, wouldn't care that part of him had been left behind. Not that day, and not Miss Lavender. His muscles clenched and he gripped the seat to turn away.

"Do you have a name?" Her voice came through his thoughts.

Anne came around to his other side and crossed her arms, glaring at him from above. Everyone seemed to enjoy being above him. She was in an unusually bristly snit that day anyway, and now she'd intercepted his chat with Miss Lavender, or rather, Miss Oleson.

"His name is stubborn. Stubborn Hammond, from *England*." She sneered the word and it grated on him. He still loved their homeland and would go back without hesitation, but not Anne, not yet. He narrowed his eyes at her and held back the retort he wanted to throw back.

Natalie giggled and held out her hand. "Pleased to make your acquaintance."

"No, you're not," Anne continued. "If you were, it wasn't my brother you met. He's as sour as the day is long."

Cody clutched his hand into a fist, the old burn scar from his escape pulling taught. He fought the rise of heat to his cheeks. He would not show his sister how she embarrassed him. He turned his gaze to Miss Oleson, avoiding his sister completely. Her mouth hung open slightly and her eyes were wide and honest. He wanted to reassure her that nothing was amiss, they simply didn't get along, but before he could, Anne spoke up again.

"It's all in fun, dear. My brother can be a little surly, so I like to remind him once in a while what it feels like to be on the receiving end. His name, in truth, is Cody Hammond." She shifted her attention to him. "Will you be joining the family for supper, Brother, or heading back to the boarding house to sulk as usual?"

He'd wanted to come, but now that she'd embarrassed him in front of Miss Oleson, it made no sense to go. He couldn't even ask her about why she was there now that Anne had spoken up for him, belittled him, in front of the stranger.

Miss Oleson leaned forward, and her green eyes caught him and held on. No one leaned in closer to him, all were repulsed. This was yet another conundrum from this strange woman. "Oh, do come. You can meet my father. He was too unwell to attend service, but he'd be so happy to meet you. You have no idea how much happiness you could bring him."

She didn't reach out and actually touch him, but it felt as if she had. Her words stopped him from refusing out of principle. She, a person who was not family, wanted him to come out to the ranch? He could find out about her enough to fill in the missing areas on his lists about her. Women like her were supposed to run away when he pushed back, not be more kind. If she acted as his list dictated, then he wouldn't need to observe her further for understanding. Then, maybe, he could understand why she didn't run from him like everyone else.

Anne shook her head and crossed her arms. "Miss Oleson, this is not a project you or your father want to take on. My brother is in no position to help anyone. Your father needs to heal, not work."

Miss Oleson ducked her chin and a few soft, brown strands of hair slid forward and partially blocked her face. He wanted to tuck them behind her ears, so he could see her better. Then he wanted to slap his own face for the trouble. What had gotten into him? When she glanced up, her eyes were glassy.

"I know you're right, Anne. It's just, I have so much hope that he'll improve. He does so love his work."

Cody slid back from the two women and into the armrest on the end of the pew. A project. She wanted him to be some sort of project for her father. Everyone was always trying to work on him, make him better. Couldn't they all understand he was just fine how he was? He took his crutch and stood, forcing Anne to step back. It would still be difficult to ride out to the ranch, but this one time he'd do it. He'd always been able to figure out a problem by looking at it long enough, but after giving the mystery of Miss Oleson a few days, he was no closer to solving it. Attending the Oleson supper would answer his questions. The lure of becoming her project would make her open up to his questions. Then, he would ask for a ride home before he could become someone else's job.

Anne glared at him for leaving Miss Oleson without giving her an answer. He sighed and sat back down in the pew, then gritted his teeth and tried to keep his face placid. "I'll join you. I wouldn't want to deny your father happiness. It sounds like he has so little." Cody stifled a smile when he heard Anne gasp next to him. He had never gone to the Sunday meal, despite weekly invitations. The only time he'd gone out to the Oleson ranch was for a party to celebrate Anne and Eli's wedding. After that, he'd stayed in town.

"You're coming, actually coming? I'll go tell Eli. I think we have room in our wagon." Anne rushed off to find her husband, leaving him once again with Miss Oleson.

"Why would your father be so glad to see me?" He relaxed slightly, now that Anne had left.

Miss Oleson softly pursed her bottom lip, but held her smile. "You see, Mr. Hammond, my father makes wooden appendages for those who have lost them. It is his joy to help those who have been cut from regular society, to get back in."

A rushing sound filled his ears and though Cody was aware she still sat there, waiting for him to respond, he couldn't. His mouth wouldn't form words, his ears wouldn't hear, his heart wouldn't listen. "Excuse me, Miss Oleson. I need a bit of air." He stood and fumbled with his crutch. To his dismay, she reached out and grabbed it before it fell to the floor and handed it to him. He couldn't even look at her to express how he felt, he just had to get away.

No one gave him a kindness, and he wouldn't accept one even if they did. The last person to give him something without a motive was Anne, and that was just before her governess had cost him everything. Kindness cost, the world always took back what was given and usually with interest. He stumbled down the steps, barely managing to stay on his feet.

"Brother!" Anne met him just outside and took his elbow. She glanced him over with concern. "We're just over here. Come, let me get you comfortable for the ride."

He stared at her and his mouth still wouldn't work of his own accord. Telling Anne he didn't want to go, and why, would be admitting why he'd never forgiven her, even after all these years. Remaining silent meant he had to face his worst fear.

CHAPTER 6

A cool breeze blew over Natalie's shoulders and she huddled a little closer to Lula in the back of the wagon on the way home from church. She'd never been embarrassed by her father's profession, had never worried about approaching someone with a need, so it had seemed natural to talk to Cody. It was a mistake, though. He'd stumbled from her without saying a word. Most were grateful for the chance to walk again, or to look somewhat normal, but Cody had been angry.

"Is something the matter, Natalie?" Lula leaned forward and tugged on her daughter's hair to get her to stop hitting her brother.

"I think I said something offensive to Mr. Hammond. He almost ran from me in church." She flinched at her own choice of words and prayed Lula wouldn't think her rude.

"Cody doesn't like anyone who isn't his sister and he doesn't even like her all that much. He's just that way. Though, he is cordial to women, to most men he can barely hide his disdain. It's most apparent around men who ride horses." She glanced about the wagon. Though each man seemed to ignore the conversation, all frowned slightly.

"Do you suppose it's a touch of jealously?" Natalie had never met a man with a missing limb quite like Mr. Hammond. Usually they were so pleased to have her attention for a while and were thankful to have her listen to their stories, then grateful to receive help. Mr. Hammond didn't seem to want her to even come near him.

"I don't know what it is and it isn't anything he would willingly share. Anne might have some idea, but I don't even think she tries anymore. He's had a few rough patches that led him to America. He's been through things a lot harder than just losing part of his leg."

Everyone else in the wagon started up their own quiet conversations, prompting Natalie to keep talking. If others were listening, she wouldn't want to talk about Cody and make people think she was more concerned with him than was right. "If that's the case, why doesn't he seek out a friend, someone he can talk to?"

Lula laughed softly and finally picked her daughter up and plopped the child on her lap, kicking the whole way. "He doesn't because most men don't, not intentionally. They may bring up something with another man to work out an idea in their head, but they don't usually go to another man for anything emotional. And from what Anne has said, he's had a lot to deal with. I think if he were closer with his sister, he wouldn't be nearly so gruff, but he has no woman to listen and he won't allow any women near him, so he stays just where he is."

He'd chosen to come out after church. According to the whispered words among the Olesons, that in itself was a battle won. Cody seemed to keep to himself, which wasn't odd from others like him. But usually, when given the chance to have a friendly ear, others would take it. "Why do you think he decided to come today?" It wasn't her, he'd run from her at the mention of a wooden leg to make him whole again.

"Only Cody knows that for certain. You could ask him. As I said, he is generally less snappish to women, though he has no love for us. My husband and his brothers have left Cody alone almost since he came, just because they don't see any hope of changing him. Izzy mentioned to Conrad that she would like to bring Cody some sweets to see if he might settle down a bit, but Conrad asked her not to. Not until Cody shows that he can have gratitude. Otherwise, it's wasted."

Natalie had never heard of wasted grace or kindness before. It was possible that was all Cody was missing. If no one gave him anything, how would he learn to give it in return? She'd found, shortly after Mama died, when kindness and love were in short supply in her little family, that giving something away often brought healing. When Father gave away one of his wooden limbs, for a short time, life was better. He would be nicer, listen more, care about the boys and their schooling. Once that happiness wore off, they would go back to the way things were. Wounds needed time to heal, but kindness seemed to multiply once it had been shared.

"I wouldn't mind listening to his story," Natalie mused. "If he would let me."

Lula nodded slightly, then pursed her lips. "You just might get your chance. Cody is used to going back to the boarding house after Sunday service and it's quiet there on a Sunday afternoon. He has no idea what is waiting for him out at the ranch. He'll probably go hide in Maretta's sun room. That's where you'll find him."

Natalie tried to remember the various rooms in the large Oleson home. Though she was grateful they had enough space for her father, herself, and her brothers, learning all the rooms had taken a few days. She would watch Mr. Hammond when they arrived and if she found him alone, she could test her idea. Everyone needed a listening ear.

The wagons pulled to a stop in front of the big white house and people poured out from them, all eighteen of them, including Lula's two very small children and Izzy's infant, Junior. Natalie's brothers broke from the group and headed for the bunkhouse, waving to the others as they left.

"They just can't seem to ever mind," she mumbled as she climbed over the box of the wagon and down the wheel. Barton didn't touch her, but stood by her side in case she fell.

"We invited them, just so you know. Each one has a chip on their shoulder, just waiting for the right person to dare and knock it off. Conrad is pretty busy with his new family at the moment, but this won't go beyond his notice. He takes his job of oldest pretty seriously."

She shook her head and took a deep breath, praying for a little calm. "Hopefully he has better luck with them than I did. The Good Lord knows I tried."

Her poor mama would turn in her grave if she saw how her sons had turned out. The oldest, John, was the leader. Natalie often thought if she could turn his heart, the others might follow, but it wasn't her responsibility any longer.

Yelling from behind her drew her attention and she turned to see Barton attempting to help Cody from the wagon.

"I'm just trying to help you." Barton struggled to keep Cody from falling to the ground.

"I don't need your help. I've lived long enough without you or anyone else. Let me be," Cody retorted.

"You're such a stubborn, rude—"

Acid burned in Natalie's stomach and she couldn't stand to listen to another word. Somewhere beneath the bluster was a man just like all the others she'd known her whole life.

"Stop!" She rushed up to the men. "Barton, let him try. There's no need to take a man's pride. Just stand by like you did with me. If he needs your help, he'll ask."

Barton set Cody down and backed away from the wagon, but they'd gained an audience now. Cody stared at her, his jaw slightly slack. In the sun, his hair had stripes of blue, like a crow's feathers. When he didn't move, the family around them took to doing other things until most had gone into the house, leaving Cody, Barton and Natalie outside.

"Barton, why don't you take care of the horses? I'll get down all on my own." Cody stared ahead, as if he'd been waiting for everyone to disperse.

Barton shook his head, but went to one of the other wagons to start unhitching. Cody glanced down at her. "Willing to hold this for me?" He handed her his crutch and she took it silently.

He turned around in the seat with no back, and lowered himself to the wagon bed. When he'd gotten his leg out in front of him, he maneuvered to the lip of the wagon, reached over the box and slid the box rod to free the back board. Once it was laying flat, he pushed his leg out the back then lowered his leg over the edge. With a little hop off the back, he landed on his solid leg and caught himself. She handed him his crutch and he took it with a nod. "Thank you." He adjusted his rounded hat more squarely on his head then brushed himself off with his free hand.

She'd expected him to be warmer after she'd defended him, but it wasn't meant to be. He nodded slightly at her, then headed into the house. Cody was going to be harder to crack than any of her other *missing men*. She'd called them that because no other name seemed to fit. Part of them was missing, but they could be whole again. Cody could be whole again. If only he'd let her help.

Barton led two horses to the barn, leaving her alone. She'd never been in a group so large as the Oleson family, and since Cody hadn't wanted to stay outside and talk with her as she'd hoped, she had no desire to go inside. Her father would need her soon, but she didn't want to have to dodge through all the people to get to him. Natalie approached the next set of horses and rubbed the nose of the lead horse.

She would've gladly gone inside if there was anyone in there waiting to see her or give her something to do, but she'd been kept from all chores except her father. "Sometimes there's just too many people, and not enough, all in the same room."

The horse raised its head, but offered nothing in the way of a solution. At least it didn't walk away like Cody had.

CHAPTER 7

Noise seemed to follow Cody through the house and he needed somewhere quiet to think. Miss Lavender had come to his defense and that had been yet another unexpected event. Would she never do as he thought she would? He always thought about the possibilities of a situation before joining in and that hadn't been one. Few people surprised him, those were usually people of extreme faith who seemed to do very illogical things. Most people were predictable, relatable, forgettable.

He wandered to a seat in the far corner of the little sitting room right in the front where he'd come in. Most of the family had migrated to the back of the house near the kitchen. Though there were some wonderful scents coming from that direction, he just couldn't join them yet. He had to work out in his mind why Miss Oleson would come to his defense. There was no other way to be certain he wouldn't become just another pet dog to her, like Langerford thought of him at the bank.

He might feed or care for abandoned dogs and cats

when they visited him behind the boarding house, but Cody had no intention of becoming one. Just like those cast-off dogs, he wasn't wanted. It was easier to relate to the animals who came begging. But, he wouldn't beg. Not from his sister, nor the irritatingly unexpected woman.

Miss Lavender wandered out in front of the house, taking her time, as if she didn't want to enter the party any more than he did. Through the window, he couldn't hear her, but he could see her mouth moving, talking to herself, as she slowly moved between flower bushes, then over to the wide circle fence of the corral. She'd worn lavender when he'd met her, but today she wore a deep blue dress. It was a narrow cut, making her look taller than he'd thought she was originally, but it was an illusion. He'd stood next to her outside and she'd only reached just above his shoulder.

As if she felt his eyes on her, she turned and glanced about, her lips a pretty rose color against her light skin.

"Staring at anything in particular, Brother?" Anne wandered into the room and sat in a chair across from him.

Blast. Anne had gained much in the way of pluck since she'd married. Before, she would leave him be when he wanted it. Now, even his best scowl wasn't working.

"I was looking for a quiet little corner. It isn't as if your family truly wants me here."

"That's where you're wrong," she said. "You *are* my family and I want you here. I want you to be happy, even if I don't quite remember what that looks like. I want you to smile like you did before the war."

"Stop." He couldn't have her continue and make him so angry that he would slip up and release all he'd worked so hard to keep penned up inside. Let her think it was the loss of his leg that had turned him sour. Let her think there was no hope he might change, because there was no getting his leg back, nor was there room for forgiveness of his sister.

"Stop, go, stay, yield, quiet. All you have to say to me anymore are one-word commands. It's like we were when you first returned after losing your leg, still unable to use the crutch until I started wheeling you around. Did you forget, Brother, that it was me that pulled you out of this the first time? I can't do it this time. I'm not resilient enough to bear your burdens. You'll have to find someone stronger."

She hadn't pushed him out of anything. She'd only pushed him into an asylum. "There is nothing wrong with me. I have a roof over my head and food. I'd be happy to see my sister once a week, but instead, she forces me to go to church to see her even though she works in town every day. Why should I change?"

"Why?" Anne raised an eyebrow and glanced out the window. "Because I've also seen the need in your eyes when there's a wedding service at the church. I've watched the look on your face when Barton gives Lula a kiss as he helps her out of the wagon at church. You want more for yourself, even if you never admit it, and I wish I could be the one to help you, but I can't. You hate me for some reason I can't figure out and I can't break past that this time."

"I think you have an excellent imagination," he ground out the words past his teeth. He hadn't planned to divulge so much and especially not to her, but he couldn't keep his eyes from drifting out to Miss Lavender, still standing by the fence. Thrice she'd been kind to him and he simply had no way to respond to it.

Anne glanced out the window and the side of her lip raised slightly. "So, there's that longing look once more. At least there's still hope."

Miss Oleson came through the door and glanced over the room. As soon as her eyes met his, she tucked her chin and turned to dash towards the stairs.

"Natalie, wait!" Anne called.

Cody flinched, knowing that his plan to avoid Miss Oleson was about to be ruined. His sister managed to ruin everything, he shouldn't be surprised.

Natalie turned and Anne invited her over to sit. She hesitated a moment, then sat on the other end of the sofa from where he sat. "You wanted something, Mrs. Oleson?"

"Call me Anne, everyone else does. Yes, I wanted to apologize to you and to my brother for my rude interruption at the church. You two were about to have a talk and I cut in. It was quite impolite of me. I'll leave you both to start over, without my help." Anne stood and gave him a sharp glance, then left.

Miss Oleson felt a mile away at the end of the couch, though it was only a few feet. He turned slightly, so he didn't face away from her. She sat on the edge of the seat, her back straight, and peeked at him every few seconds. He could just as well have been a black bear for how she glanced at him. Was he really so terrifying as that?

"Um," he searched for what to say, but his mouth had gone completely dry. He couldn't even think of anything to drive her from the room and he was usually quite good at that.

"You can call me Natalie." She blinked softly at him.

Kindness number four—he was lost.

CHAPTER 8

Confusion drew Cody's brows together and Natalie couldn't guess what had caused it. She'd only offered her name. His cranky way had endeared him to her somewhat. At least she now understood what to expect from him and that could only help her in convincing him to let her make him a leg.

"Unless you don't want to, that is." She clasped her hands in her lap to keep herself from fidgeting. This man was so different from all her other *missing men*. Why couldn't he just act as all of them and be friendly, let her listen to his rueful story, and then let her father provide them with joy? Yes, they did charge a fee—she and her family had to live—but most of the men were glad for not only the wooden limb, but the chance to be who'd they'd been before.

Cody slid forward in the seat and turned to face her more fully. "Natalie, thank you. You may call me Cody, although I doubt you'll find much reason to call me anything."

His voice was warm, like the sun on a rock at a swimming hole with a slight accent that some in New England affected when they wanted to sound important, though she had a feeling he wasn't putting on airs. It was just the way he spoke. He certainly didn't aim to impress her. She turned to face him and the gap between them seemed less cavernous. "Thank you. I'm sorry if my presence makes you uncomfortable. I can leave if you wish."

He laughed, but it held no humor, more of a closely guarded sadness that tore at her heart. "You are an Oleson. You belong here. *I* do not."

But they had invited him. Surely there had been reason to. The Olesons must enjoy his company, or they wouldn't have gone to the trouble. "On the contrary. At least you were invited, I just showed up unannounced." She laughed, hoping it would bring some light back to his gray eyes.

"Why were you in such a hurry to get here? I've been curious about that since you came in." His eyes broke contact with hers for the slightest of seconds and she leaned closer to him. He fidgeted with the sleeve of his shirt and she smiled at the idea that he hadn't meant to admit that.

"I was in a hurry because my father is gravely ill. I wasn't sure I would make it here with him and my brothers were almost no help. I hadn't warned Nathan we were coming, so they weren't watching for us. I had to leave Father alone in the wagon to go speak to you. Even though they were on horseback and could easily dismount, they didn't." She tried so hard to be kind to everyone, but her brothers had used up all her compassion. She frowned for a moment and directed her thoughts back to his question. "I couldn't leave Father sitting up in the wagon for too long. I was worried he might fall."

Cody slid a little closer to her on the couch and her heart rejoiced. He was opening up to her. She could feel the warmth building ever so slightly between them.

"We brothers can be a hard lot. Men often do things that don't make much sense to anyone but us. I'm sure I vex my sister horribly. Of course, I can't say I don't try."

It had never occurred to her that they might do things without the intent she took from their actions. It seemed as if they gave her a bad turn no matter what. "I'm certain they try as well. I just want them to act their age. Mama died just as many years ago for them as for me and I've had to shoulder all the burden." She'd meant to get his story, listen to him, but he'd managed to pull her story from her. And not just any part, the part she usually held closest to her heart.

His face shifted slightly and his arms relaxed. She rejoiced inside at the small battle won so quickly.

"I'm sorry. My family was also torn apart, but not by death." Cody's voice calmed her and the anger over her brothers that had begun to take over subsided.

"I'm sorry, losing family is horrible." She faced the loss of yet another and probably soon. Tears pricked her eyes and she blinked to keep them at bay. This hard man would not understand her tears.

He sat up straight and shrank away from her. It took all her might not to reach for his lapels and pull him back.

"Yes, it is very difficult." He shoved his crutch under his arm and used it to quickly push himself off the couch. "I'm sorry, Natalie. I asked Anne to call you over to tell you that I have no desire to be your pet project. You will have to find someone else to make your father happy."

In a few moments she found herself alone in the

sitting room. Cody kept running from her, but she got the feeling he was running from himself more. His mention of her father only proved it. He was trying to defend himself against her, against the hurt that might come if her father couldn't help him.

She dashed outside and ran to the bunkhouse. Though she'd been told not to go into the building, because it was full of men, she had to talk to her brothers. After a quick knock, John came to the door.

He cocked his head and stared down at her, his deep blue eyes so different from her own. All her brothers had taken after Father, while she'd taken after their mother. It both bothered and comforted her because she could look into a mirror and remember Mama, but her brothers and father had only to look at her to be reminded of what they'd lost. In some ways, it was how she clutched that connection with the woman she'd lost far too soon. For some, a mirror was vanity. To her, it was comfort.

"John, can I talk to you and the others?"

He leaned back into the long building. "Charles, George, we're needed outside."

Her brothers met her a few feet outside and she glanced at each one, so alike, yet so different. Charles was her defender in a pinch, always coming to her rescue, but he also gave her the hardest time. He wanted to play, not mind. George was the youngest and a prankster. If he was anyone but her brother, she would think he was a little weasel.

"I need your help, please. There's a man—"

"We noticed," John finished. "How long do you need the log to be?"

She hadn't considered that. Usually, she was able to get measurements. They never gave a limb as a surprise, in case it didn't fit properly. In Cody's case, they would need not only the tibia section, but the knee and foot as well. "I'd say, three independent sections, the longest of which is roughly sixteen inches."

"You don't know? You didn't measure?" John stared down at her, then turned to glance all around them. "Have you taken note of how sparse the trees are here? You might want to measure before you go sending us out to find something strong enough. You might not get two chances."

She already knew that, and it wasn't because of the wood. Father might not even be able to complete the limb and she would have to finish it. "Please, just do this."

He slid his hand down his face and his gaze flicked to the sky as he widened his stance. "Nat, this place, this is our chance. We've been talking and all of us could really fit in here. Pa never wanted us to follow in his footsteps, so he never taught us anything except how to gather the right wood. He didn't even teach us how to shape it, much less make the attachments and joints. This will be the last time we go out for you, because we intend to ask Conrad for jobs."

She stared into eyes that she'd been sure were hard a moment before, but now just wanted her approval. "I think that's a fine idea."

John nodded and turned to his brothers. A moment later they went back into the bunkhouse without another word to her. They didn't need their older sister anymore. All she had to do now was make sure her father got strong enough to make one more limb, and make sure Cody was ready to receive the gift of freedom. After that, no one would need her at all.

CHAPTER 9

At the table, Cody sat between his sister and Maretta Oleson. Across the table sat Natalie. She remained patient, quietly waiting, yet her gaze didn't linger on him often. She seemed quite focused on the hall that led to the upstairs portion of the house. Though he knew where the stairs were, he'd never been up there and could only assume that was where her sick father lay.

The giant bowls of food began with Nathan at the head of the table, then passed to his wife and so on. Though there was always plenty of food by the time the bowls reached Natalie, she took very little. Maretta took note.

"Natalie, dear. You won't ever fill your plate if you don't take a little bit more." She picked up a bowl of sweet potatoes and handed them back to her, then a bowl still half-full of corn.

"No, thank you, ma'am." Natalie set both back on the table and bowed her head. Everyone at the table waited for Nathan to offer grace and the room went silent as he began. Cody only half-listened. He'd almost gotten drawn into Natalie's little lasso, but he wouldn't be fooled again. She was a cunning adversary, knocking him off his pedestal of understanding before quashing him with her smile. But not again.

When they finished the short prayer, conversation started up immediately and it was so loud Cody couldn't make out what any group was talking about enough to join in. Anne laid her hand over his arm and he turned from watching Natalie for a moment to listen.

"Thank you for coming, Cody. It means a lot to me. I've been married for over three months now and was beginning to think you didn't care. I know you agreed to stay in America, but it hasn't been easy for you. I know your first love is England."

Almost imperceptibly, Natalie raised her brows and her eyes darted from the stairs, to him and his sister, then back. If she was listening, what could she be curious about? It was another piece to the puzzle, and he loved a challenge.

"It's not that I don't care, Anne. You left England—you left *me*—without so much as looking back. I was sore for a while, but I'm here now. I would think that's enough." Even though it wasn't really. He didn't want to be near his sister or hear about her happiness. He didn't want to see her soft blushes as Eli whispered to her. He didn't want her unhappy, it just chaffed to see her so happy after what she'd done in his life. He'd wanted to take her with him back to England, to make her live the life she'd promised him before he was sent away. He clutched his fingers into his palm, the pain a reminder of what he'd escaped.

"I didn't know where you were and I was compelled to leave," she hissed. "We've talked about this."

It embarrassed her to talk about what happened in England. He still didn't know exactly what she'd been through, but her husband did. Eli leaned forward and gave him a quelling look.

"You brought it up, Anne." Though she hadn't really, he liked to pester her. But when he raised his eyes, Natalie glared at him for his trouble and he knew he'd gone too far.

"Anne, tell us about working in the clinic." Natalie finally picked up her fork but didn't move to take a bite of anything.

He gritted his teeth. Anne's nursing position was because of him. He'd pushed her to do something, anything, to replace him in the military. She'd refused to dress as a man and carry a gun, so she studied nursing instead. Looking back, it was foolish for him to even ask that of her, but she'd been so willing to do anything for her brother back then. Anything to make less of the pain of his loss. Except telling Mother before it was too late and firing her governess.

"It really isn't all that interesting and most of what I do is not fit for table conversation."

Natalie smiled slightly and her narrow shoulders straightened, as if she'd suddenly become comfortable sitting there, when she hadn't been before. "I am not a nurse, but I help those with medical conditions as well. My father does most of the work, but he's taught me how. We make wooden limbs for those who have lost theirs."

The table went silent as if everyone decided to hold their breath all at once. All eyes at the table focused on Natalie and on Cody. He wasn't well-liked, he knew that, but did they really expect him to be rude in their home? Would they be disappointed if he didn't let the young woman know her conversation was rude with him sitting right there?

Since it appeared the discussion was not going to continue until he responded, Cody cleared his throat and tried to be as civil as he was able. "I'm sure many of those you help are quite grateful." He went back to his roast pork and waited for the table to resume chatting.

"Interesting that you should say that, Mr. Hammond. I have yet to meet one that wasn't." She took on a rather smug smile and, as pretty as he thought her to be, he was sure at this point he could predict the course of her conversation.

"You keep in contact with those who you've helped?" he asked.

He set his fork down, no longer hungry. Others at the table shifted uncomfortably. Anne reached for his arm, but thought better of it midway and drew it back to her lap. The prospect of another leg was intriguing, but not as charity. Just like he hated being the little trick dog at the bank, he resented that Natalie would try to treat him like one of the abandoned dogs he took in.

She fidgeted in her seat at his question. "No, I can't say that I have. We travel so much that there's no way we could. How would anyone know how to reach us?"

A little voice whispered to him to hold back, to stay his opinion and keep from dashing her hopes, but he couldn't. She had brought this on herself by brashly stating why she was there. "So, it is possible that the people you have helped realized after you left that it wasn't much help at all?"

She stood from the table, her eyes glistening. "No, Mr. Hammond. It's not possible. My father does a fine job. No one would ever turn away one of his limbs. I had wanted to give you the gift of freedom from your crutches in the hopes that it would free you from the hatred in your heart as well, but I can see that no matter what, you wouldn't be grateful." She pushed in her chair and ran from the room.

Nathan cleared his throat and those who had gone silent at the outburst made to continue their talking.

Anne sighed heavily next to him and finally managed to touch his arm. "Perhaps we should take you home?"

He wasn't even sure why he'd bothered to come. It wasn't as if he was wanted there, nor did he want to be there. He stood and nodded his thanks to Nathan as he limped toward the door.

CHAPTER 10

Natalie paced back and forth at the foot of her father's bed, fuming. She'd planned to do that man a kindness and he'd treated her just as he treated his sister, with utter cold disdain. "How am I ever going to find someone to help Father now?" She flexed her hands and shook the tension from them.

"Help me with what?" Her father's warm voice came from the bed.

She hadn't heard him speak with such strength in days. The voyage had so worn him out that he'd slept most of the last few days, hardly even waking to eat. She ran over to the bed and sat, gripping his hands in hers. "It doesn't matter just now. How are you feeling?"

He chuckled softly. "I feel plum tuckered." He glanced around the room, his eyes lingering on the lace curtains. "We made it. It's still hard to believe after all the traveling. I wasn't sure we would. How are the boys handling themselves?"

She pursed her lips and tried to think of a list of things to tell him, but none of them were important enough to pester him with. "They are fine, even talking about asking their cousin Conrad for jobs." At least that news would do her father good and hopefully make him forget she'd never actually given her promise to stop making prosthetics.

"Jobs? That would do them some good. Teach them a trade. Something they can do that won't take them everywhere. And nowhere." Father rubbed his old knotty hands together. "Girl, I aimed to make you promise me you wouldn't take up my trade when I'm gone and I meant it. It's not the kind of thing you can settle down and do. I won't have you driving all over, looking for people, alone. Don't make me worry that you'll do that once I'm gone. Reassure me. Promise me."

A promise was binding. Her father had never asked for them, because no one ever knew what the future might hold and a promise was something you did not break. A marriage was the only promise her father had taught her to look forward to, though it seemed out of the question now. She was in her late twenties and had never known anyone long enough to forge a friendship, let alone something deeper. It seemed unlikely she would manage to find a husband before her years of childrearing would be over.

"I can't do that, Father. How else will I make my way?"

He shook his head, his wispy hair falling in his eyes. "That was why I insisted we come here. There will always be a place for you with my brother. I knew that even though Nathan and I hadn't spoken, even if he turned me away, he wouldn't turn you and your brothers away. He's a good man."

"So are you, Father, and you're not dead yet. Stop acting as if you've got one foot in the grave." She couldn't bear the thought of losing him. Not yet. She wasn't ready.

A ragged cough took him and she hurried to the pitcher in the corner for a glass of water. Once she made it back to him, she held it to his lips until he was able to drink.

He handed her back the cup and sighed. "Then I will have to worry about you until I'm gone and give you over to the saints to worry about."

She flinched and licked her lips. She would be all alone if she left. Her brothers would not come along. However, if he managed to get better, she wouldn't have to. "If you would force me into a promise, then I will do the same to you. There is a man here in Belle Fourche who is missing most of one leg. He is the stubbornest man I've ever met and doesn't want our help."

Father tilted his head and regarded her for a moment. "Why does it matter that he's stubborn and what are you asking of me?"

She'd thought that dealing with her brothers for the last few years would prepare her for men like Cody, but it hadn't. His words had crawled under her skin and made her more livid than her brothers could. "It matters because he needs our help."

"Only if he wants it, Natalie. You can't make a man take a step."

That wasn't what her father was supposed to say. She'd expected him to want to help, to ask her to bring him to this man to talk.

"Have you given up completely?" If he had, that meant in his own mind he was preparing to die and she had to convince him otherwise. He couldn't just prepare the way and then go as he'd done for the travel to South Dakota.

"It isn't so much giving up as it is relinquishing control. You know that I can't add a single day to my life, child. If the Lord says it's my time, it is."

She huffed at his words. The Lord was Good, that's what she'd been taught, and a good God wouldn't take away both her parents. Not when she still needed one. "I would think He could wait a little while yet."

Father reached out and caressed her cheek. "My dear Natalie. So much like your mother. Impetuous. To a fault."

She bristled under his words. "And what of my brothers? If I'm impetuous—the one who has been planning, thinking, cooking, cleaning the sites after we've stopped, and driving the wagon, what of them?" She wanted to stand, to stomp to the other side of the room. He'd called her unthinking, yet she'd done little else.

"Your brothers are young and don't know how to help you because *their* help has never been good enough for you. You were forced to act as a mother before you had the wisdom and maturity to do so."

She spun around and opened her mouth to defend herself, but he held up his hand for quiet.

"You did everything you could, and much more than you should've had to. I'm proud of you, Natalie. But you do assume, you do tend to race after a goal without thinking it through first, and you do tend to get angry with your brothers when they don't do things just so. I'm guessing that's why this man's mulishness bothers you so much. Do his ideas go against your own?"

She crossed her arms and bit her lip hard to keep from pouting. "Well, of course he doesn't agree with me or I wouldn't think he was an obstinate fool. If he agreed with me, I would think him determined and loyal." Which is just how she wanted her father to see her.

"This man does have me curious. Other than your brothers, you usually bear no ill will toward anyone. Who is this man that he's turned you so quickly to dislike?"

She turned back to face her father and hoped that he didn't think poorly of her for her thoughts on Cody. "He is the brother to Cousin Eli's wife."

"And what caused him to be crippled?"

At least Father was now interested, instead of talking about death. "I don't know. I've only spoken to him a few times."

Father laughed. "That settles it. Any man who can make you so angry you're ready to pull out your hair after just a few meetings is a man I want to meet."

Natalie smiled to herself. If anyone could get through to Cody, it was her father. He'd gotten through to the men they had helped for years. Cody wouldn't even know he'd been turned to her side until it was good and done.

CHAPTER 11

Every problem had a solution. Cody stared down at his notes on the registry desk in front of him. It had been a slow Monday at the bank and he'd had ample time to think of all the things he'd said to both Anne and to Natalie, and how they'd responded. None of it added up.

Everything he did needed to be orderly, whether it was work or kinships. There was reason in everything, yet he couldn't account for Natalie's persistence in wanting to help him, especially when he continued to give her ample reason not to. He stared down at his list of what had happened and how she *should've* reacted. Yet, even after he'd driven her from the room—though that hadn't been his intent either—she'd followed that with something again completely unexpected.

His gaze wandered to the little note laying in the upper corner of his workspace. Almost hidden. He hadn't wanted to share it with anyone, lest they think he had some connection to Natalie when he most certainly did not. She had written him a note and sent it with Anne, doing yet again, the opposite of what he'd been certain she would do, which was to let him be.

Dear Mr. Hammond,

I'm sorry for pressing you. I did not mean to make you uncomfortable. My father is quite unwell and I truly believed making you something that would remain after he is gone would give him some sort of joy, peace.

I know it isn't an easy task for you to come out to the ranch, but I would like to invite you out for a meal, since it is because I left so abruptly that you felt you had to leave before the meal was even finished on Sunday. I owe you at least that much and I own my behavior, which was neither pleasant nor acceptable.

Again, I am sorry for my rash actions and I pray that it did you no harm.

Cordially,
Natalie Oleson

He hadn't expected an invitation to return, nor her taking the blame for his prodding. He'd intended to get her mad enough to leave off, not run off. He'd fully expected Nathan to take him outside and tell him to keep his opinions *and* himself in town where they belonged, but he hadn't. Nathan had followed Anne outside and wished him well. Anne had hitched up a buggy that was built to hold just two. It was lower to the ground and easier for him to get in. He'd waited the whole ride for her to get angry with him and tell him he'd been rude. Instead, she kissed him on the cheek and told him he would see her the following week.

When she'd returned the next day, with her little white hat on proclaiming her station, he'd flinched. Usually, the hat made him uncomfortable anyway, but he'd assumed she'd finally do the sensible thing and tell him what a jack mule he was and that he could take himself right back to his beloved England because he wasn't good enough for Belle Fourche, or her family. Instead, she'd handed him the note, smiled at him—making him feel even worse—and wished him a good day.

"Hammond," Mr. Langerford called, "in here, now."

Langerford would give him the response he craved, the ability to stay one step ahead because *he* followed predictable rules, unlike everyone else in Cody's life at the moment. He reached for his crutch and slid it under his arm, his muscles protesting for a moment and he winced at the sharp pain. The skin under his arm had recently become hard and the padding of his crutch sometimes hurt. He tried to shift the position, but if he did that the crutch did no good and he had to hop. Though he could, it was silly, and he'd rather use the crutch and hurt than appear foolish.

Once he sat in Langerford's office, he rested the crutch against the desk and waited for his boss to come up with the latest test. That seemed to be the only reason he ever got pulled from his station.

"I want you to do something out of the ordinary today, Hammond. The lumber yard is looking to expand, and they want to apply for a loan. I want you to deliver this paperwork and answer any questions they might have."

Cody glanced down at his lap and took a deep breath. He was perfectly capable of walking across town, but he tended to only do it when he could do many things at once, so he only had to walk once in the span of a few days. Making an extra walk that couldn't be combined with anything else was a use of energy he wouldn't normally expend.

"Your delivery boy quit?" He kept the rough edge from his voice, barely.

Langerford laughed. "No, I want you to get used to the idea that there's more to this bank than those bars and the dollars and coins you count. There's more even than the ledgers or the watch you keep over everyone who walks in the door. The bank is about keeping up just enough of a wall so people don't feel comfortable, but open enough that they must come in."

"I thought you wanted me to be more friendly." He changed his tactic. There had to be someone better suited to go all the way across town.

"More friendly than a grizzly with cubs, yes. As friendly as a puppy, no." He slid a sheaf of papers across his desk and a messenger bag.

"What's that?" Cody had never seen the usual bank delivery boy use anything to carry the papers in.

"I want your hand available to shake, not holding paperwork. Use it." He stared at Cody, challenging him to question him more.

His mind clicked to life, looking for options. He didn't have to think of everything, to figure a way out.

"While you're down that way, your sister asked me to send you over to see her this morning. She said she'd noticed your crutch needed some mending and she brought lunch for two."

He'd been outwitted by the banker and his sister, blamed if he didn't both want to growl in anger and shake the man's hand. Not many had been able to completely pull the wool over his eyes for a long time. Now he could go do the job and he had another reason to go across town, making it worthwhile. Not to mention,

Anne might be able to fix whatever had worn away on his crutch, causing his arm to be so sore.

"Sure, I'll do your little errand. Today." By tomorrow, he would be able to work out reasons why it wouldn't happen again, but today Langerford would get his way.

CHAPTER 12

John wasn't in the bunkhouse like he was supposed to be. George and Charles didn't know where he'd gone, or what he was up to. Father was sleeping, so Natalie couldn't go to him and ask what could be done about her missing brother. Her cousins were all off doing their chores about the ranch. With a helpless weight hanging in her stomach, she turned to head back to the house after her fruitless search.

She'd planned to tell John to wait in getting wood because Father would talk to Cody, convince him, then they could measure him properly and he might be the last man to get one of her father's useful works of art. At least, she thought of them that way. Some who made prosthetic limbs used rough and crude methods, often they looked very little like real limbs and their function was mediocre. Her father had despised that. He'd developed a way to do it better.

Each piece that was missing, was represented in the

limb. Though, without muscles, he'd never figured out how to make them movable without forcing the wearer to drag his leg. That had been his life's goal, but he hadn't managed to find a way, yet. That was another reason the Lord couldn't take him yet. The world needed his expertise.

Charles followed her up the few steps to the porch. "Sit with me, Sister."

It wasn't a request as much as a command and she itched to ignore him, but of the brothers, she got along with him the best. He gently took her elbow and led her over to the swing. She'd been fussing over him for so long, she'd forgotten that he was only five years younger than her. It had seemed like so many when they were children, and even more when they had gone through the awkward years. Now, he stood tall and strong, in charge. She'd been there the whole time, but had somehow missed that he'd become a man.

"What is it? Have you thought of somewhere John might be?" She'd just been to the barn to ask, but John hadn't been there.

"No. I wanted to ask what your plans are? We both know Father won't last forever. Do you plan to stay here, or take the wagon and keep going?" His hard blue eyes bore into hers, yet his shoulders were relaxed. He wasn't angry with her, just curious. She'd thought Father had talked to all of them about staying in Belle Fourche, but she had yet to really give her word.

"Haven't you talked to Father recently?" Why were her brothers forever doing things to vex her? His question could have been answered if he'd just listened.

"Yes, but he doesn't tell us anything. He keeps thinking that you tell us whatever he says like you always have, so he doesn't have to."

She bit her lip. How long had he been doing that, and how long had she blamed them for having to repeat things and assuming they just hadn't listened? "Father asked me to make a promise that I would not. Though I avoided directly making the promise, it is his wish that I stay here."

"But will you?" He stared off toward the pasture, and she didn't feel accused. Had she put her brothers off so much that they hesitated to talk to her?

"If I give my word, I'll keep it. Though, I have to say, I can't see that I have much reason to stay. I'm twenty-eight years old and have virtually no talents."

"A woman who is good with woodworking isn't talentless." He chuckled. You can do with a knife what many men only wish they could. I'm glad you're staying. I wouldn't want to have to worry where you were going, and I'd rather stay here."

"Charles?" She stopped him as he stood to leave. "Would you have followed me, if I had chosen to go?"

He sighed and took one step down. "I don't rightly know. I'm glad you aren't asking me to make that choice. It's nice here. Lots of space and no need to move on."

She'd hated to admit that she'd enjoyed that part too. Traveling could be exciting, or hard work. They'd seen both sides of the coin. "I know John is happy to stay, what of George?" He was tough to read. He always had a scheme to pull, usually on her, but she'd hardly laid eyes on him since they'd arrived.

"He's the same George as always, just now he targets some of the men in the bunkhouse. Most don't pay him any mind. He's still young yet. Has a lot to learn.

Natalie let him leave and pushed the swing back with her feet and let it sway forward. In the span of less than a week, she'd lost the only work she'd ever had, lost her place as the leader of her brothers, lost her ability to talk to *missing men*, and lost her place as George's main target. A knot formed in her throat and she closed her eyes against it.

God is good and He will provide...

Mother had said that to her every night at prayer time. She clung to the phrase, it was a connection to both her mother and the Lord. He had to provide a place for her, something to keep her hands busy, a healing in her father. All this He had to provide.

In her pocket, she kept a small knife. Though she usually preferred to use a whittle and chisel on wood when she started anything, all she had on her was her knife. Just off the porch was a small willow tree and she smiled, remembering the very first thing her father taught her how to make.

She leaned over the rail and, finding a limb that was just about thick enough, so it was no longer flexible, sawed it off with her knife. She cut the piece a little longer than her hand, then sliced a notch in it. Just a bit back from the notch, she carefully made a slice all the way around about a half inch behind the notch, then took the portion she'd cut off and tapped the cut wood all up and down it to loosen the bark. After sliding the bark from the center, she deepened the notch, then slid the bark tube back on.

She'd made so many whistles like that to practice holding a knife, her brothers had actually grown weary of them. The little instrument fit against her lips and, with a sharp blow, produced a high-pitched call that sent birds in the trees flying. It was a child's toy, but instead of bringing joy, it reminded her that Mother had been there when she'd made her last one, and that she would never pass on how to make one to any of her own children.

She tucked both the knife and the whistle back in her pocket. Remembering the past and making toys wouldn't help her find John and it wouldn't find her peace. She had to leave that up to the Lord.

CHAPTER 13

Cody made it to the lumber yard, and though he was generally uncomfortable in a crowd, was glad of all the people waiting in line. It gave him a chance to rest for a minute before talking to anyone. He glanced around the store for Mr. James, the owner. Since he was busy helping others, Cody limped back outside and sat on a bench along the outer wall of the lumber yard.

One of the *new* Oleson brothers stood off a ways, picking through the cast off wood pieces, eyeing each one as if they were to be as important as a cornerstone. It was John, the oldest boy, though he didn't know if John was older than Natalie or not. He couldn't recall if she'd told him that bit of information and she didn't look to be older than her brother.

John selected and rejected a few logs, then glanced up and caught Cody's eye. The young man nodded, then went right back on to what he was doing. Cody glanced up and down the street to see if Natalie happened to be with him. Drat it all if he didn't want to see her. He had to know why she would send him that note. There had to be more to it than what she'd said. Too many variables. He rubbed his arm, but touching the area just made it itch and burn all the more.

Mr. James came outside and offered Cody a hand to stand. Cody shook it and released him quickly, not wanting help.

"Good to see you. Harvey said you'd be stopping by with my papers. Come on back." He motioned Cody back into the building.

As they walked through the store to Edgar's office, Cody noted another man had come from the mill to help people looking to buy, freeing Mr. James to talk to Cody for a minute. He didn't recognize the man, and wondered how long it would be until he knew everyone in the growing town, if ever.

"Busy in here," Cody remarked, taking a seat and pulling the messenger bag from his neck. It had flopped against his side the whole way and he was glad to be rid of it.

"Yes. Everyone in town is excited about the expansion." Edgar relaxed into his seat.

Cody dug in the bag for the thick folder of paperwork. He hadn't noticed when he'd packed it in a rush, but it was quite a bit thicker than the loan paperwork he'd seen in the past. He set the papers down on the desk and tapped them back into a straight, neat stack. He hadn't taken the time to look through them at the bank because he'd needed to leave right away to make it on time. He hated to go through paperwork he hadn't looked over. Langerford would've assumed it was fine, since Cody could do the sums in his head to check everything.

"Mr. James." He laid the papers down. "Let's get started."

Someone knocked on the door behind him and Cody turned at the interruption.

"Mr. James, sorry to bother you. Someone is here asking about the scrap lumber. What do we charge for it?"

With an annoyed glance and the wave of his hand, the door closed again and, though it was quieter, the buzz of the saws outside were still loud enough to make Cody clear his throat so he could speak louder. "I think the paperwork is all in order, but give me a moment to look through it. I didn't prepare it."

Edgar huffed. "I should say not. Mr. Langerford did. If he's having the tellers put together the loans, people will start having a problem." Mr. James narrowed his eyes and stared him down.

Cody ignored the implication that he wasn't capable of doing the job simply because he didn't have an office. He could do Langerford's job, had even been used to verify that many loans were correct. Harvey had valued his expertise. He scanned the first page, the land contract, then the building costs. At the bottom of the third page, he found a slight error. A zero had been omitted and the decimal was in the wrong place.

He hated walking back to the bank and missing Anne when she had planned to help him, but he had to get the document fixed before it could be signed. "I'm sorry. In checking this over, I've found a mistake. The interest rate was not figured properly, and you wouldn't have been charged the current rate."

James flung him a penetrating stare. "I have people ready to get started on this job, today. How long will it take to fix this issue, Hammond?"

He resented that he was being blamed for finding the error he hadn't made. If he'd had time to check the document beforehand, the error might have been corrected before Edgar even saw it. "I would hope that Langerford would get to it right away, knowing you're waiting for it. I'll point out where the error is and he'll have to do little more than copy it and figure out the last few pages."

"You'd best hurry back and make sure he does." Mr. James stood and waited for Cody to grab his crutch and slip the bag back over his head. Cody slid the papers inside, then followed Mr. James back out to the front. It was much less busy now as people dispersed to go home for the noon meal or to find a quiet place under a tree to eat.

"You've got three hours, Hammond. I'd better have those on my desk by three o'clock." Mr. James strode out into the street, his boots thudding loudly as he left.

Cody had handled the situation the only way he knew how, but it still left him angry that he'd had to at all. He should've looked over the paperwork before he left the bank and if he'd been late, at least he'd have been prepared.

It took even longer to get all the way back across town with his arm sore and now it spread to his ribcage. It burned and felt as dry and hot as baked clay. By the time he made it back to the bank, he was itching for a fight with Langerford. His boss had always impressed upon everyone that the bank was a system of checks and balances, all were supposed to help keep the system as error-free as possible.

Usually, if he hadn't been called by Langerford himself, he would ask the secretary to see if he could get in to see him, but he ignored the rule and stormed right for the door, intent on giving his boss a piece of his mind. When he shoved it open, a small blond woman with a pert nose and rosy cheeks gasped and quickly hid her face behind her hat.

"Hammond, you don't usually barge in unannounced. What seems to be the problem?" Langerford said, ignoring the woman sitting in front of him and giving his full attention to Cody.

All the steam he'd worked up vanished in light of the fact that he now looked like a boor in front of the lady and he searched for the angry words he'd practiced the entire walk back. But he couldn't be churlish in front of the woman. "The loan papers, there was a mistake on the bottom of page three. He wants them back by three this afternoon."

Cody removed the bag from around his neck and set it on the desk, catching the young woman staring at him from under her light lashes.

"Cody, this is my niece, Miss Alicia Greely."

He nodded to the woman, then directed his attention back to Langerford. "I can't walk all the way back down there today." He pressed against the pain in his shoulder. Anne might have been able to help him. Now, he'd have to wait and ask her at church. A full week away.

"That's fine. Alicia, can you take Mr. Hammond down to the clinic at the end of the street?"

The woman gasped again, but nodded quickly, the feathers on her hat dancing with the movement. She clasped her hands tightly in her lap, clutching a little black bag. He would've offered his hand, but if he helped her in his state, he might accidentally fall and pull her right to the floor.

"I'll have my runner bring the file to Mr. James at the end of the day. Thank you for letting me know. Oh, and in the future, Mr. Hammond, please knock before entering my office."

He was too tired to fight his boss and find out why he couldn't have just asked the runner to do it in the first place. It was abominable that a stranger would now be giving him a ride across town and worse, she seemed so painfully shy she'd most likely rather let the horse run her to ground than give him a ride.

She waited just outside the door to the office and he noticed how pale she seemed, even with her golden hair.

"Miss." He nodded, limping for the door. If Langerford was sending him to see Anne this late in the day, he'd just gotten the remainder of his shift off, at least that much had gone his way. He heard the tap of her boots as she followed him.

"Mr. Hammond?" Her voice was unsteady as she met him at the door.

"Yes, Miss Greely?"

"I've never driven a buggy before."

He took a deep breath. Today was, apparently, the day for firsts.

CHAPTER 14

The thump of her father's legs hitting the floor woke Natalie from her nap. She'd been resting in a rocker in the corner of his room. The last thing she'd remembered was watching the lace curtain flutter in the breeze before she'd let exhaustion take her. Normally, sitting idle would've chaffed her conscience, but her father needed her nearby.

Father glanced over at her and gave her a reassuring smile. "If I'm going to meet this young man, we'd best get on our way to town. He's not going to come to us, my girl. Get a move on."

He hadn't shown so much energy or vitality in weeks and Natalie jumped from her spot, fully awake, and she helped him dress and get ready to leave. She linked her arm with his as he slowly shuffled across the floor and to the hallway. Her father had only been through the house once, and he'd been very sick on his way to that room, but he seemed to know just where he was headed and Natalie let him lead. He might not get that many more opportunities.

Once they reached the porch, he sat slowly on one of the chairs and took a deep breath, then let it out. "You'll have to hitch the wagon or get one of your brothers. I can't do it." Admitting his frailty seemed to take more out of Papa than the walk and she didn't linger, knowing it would embarrass him for her to see him that way. He wasn't old, only fifty-five, but his life had used up his years to the full measure.

Natalie found Charles in the barn and had him hitch the wagon. Though he was skeptical of her motives and even more so when she told him Papa had asked her to. Charles followed her out of the barn, leading the horses and rig. Once Papa had taken his seat, Charles glanced up to her and conveyed much in the guarded look he gave her. *Take care of him.*

Papa sighed as he settled in next to her. "Tell me about this man. How did he become lame, or is this a defect from birth?" he asked as they rolled out onto the road that would lead to town.

She'd never been able to glean that from anyone. There hadn't been a single person willing to tell her anything about Cody, beyond that he didn't seem to want to be in Belle Fourche at all and if he could, he'd go back to England. The more walls she came up against, the more she wanted to know. Why were people so hesitant to help Cody, or even talk about him?

"I'm not sure. I think it might have been an accident. From what I've heard, he came from England and I would think traveling with a wheeled chair or even a crutch, as I've seen him use, would be very difficult at sea. It might be a recent injury. It would also explain why he doesn't want to speak on it. Fresh wound."

Her father nodded, but made no immediate reply. They had met a few men in their travels who wanted a limb to replace the one they'd recently lost, but they often struggled to talk about their injuries, the more recent the injury, the harder it seemed for them to talk about it.

"Life is rarely that easy to figure out. People have a depth and breadth wider than any ocean and a capacity to fill all of it with sentiments."

She'd just assumed he was a boor. Some would even call his behavior at the Sunday gathering rude, though those same people would probably also label *her* rude for walking out. Papa was rarely wrong when it came to motives, it helped him get through to people faster. "If you believe it, then perhaps so will I. It's merely that he's a difficult man to agree with."

Papa leaned back against the walled-in box of the wagon, and stared at the sky as he held tightly to his seat. "We've helped a great many men, Natalie. It's possible the Good Lord drew us here to help this last one. I don't think I'll be doing any more after this one."

Natalie yanked on the reins to stop the horses. She wouldn't normally do such a cruelty to the poor things, but they couldn't continue. Not until Father stopped insisting he was going to die. "There is no way you can know that. We could make many more. Look at how much better you're doing? Don't you miss roaming, finding men who need us, who need *you*?" He had to remember how important his work was, or he might just give up.

Before he could respond, her father was hit with a coughing fit that had him doubled over and shook the very seat she shared with him. He yanked his handkerchief from his pocket and held it over his mouth. She didn't miss, though he tried to hide it, the bright crimson stain on the rag when he finally finished.

"Let's meet this young man and then get back home. I'm tired," he trailed off, closing his eyes against the tears that gathered and trickled down his cheeks at the force of the coughing fit.

Natalie bit her lip as she flicked the lines to get the horses moving again. It would have to be a short trip and she wasn't even sure what she could say to Cody to get him to talk to her father, especially since he knew her plan to get him a new leg, and how. Meeting her father would give away her plan completely.

"You don't seem to like this man much, so why are you wanting to do this for him?" Her father's words were soft, as if he were trying to control the cough by being as quiet as possible.

She hadn't considered why, beyond the fact that he was the only man in town she'd met that her father could help. What she *had* figured out was that Cody could remind her father why he must get better. "He is intriguing in that he is the only man with a missing limb I've met who didn't want to talk to me or who wasn't hopeful I could help."

"So, you're drawn to the fact that he's different from any man you've met before?" Her father continued to question her. There was more to it than what he was asking, but she couldn't understand. There wasn't any more to her curiosity about Cody Hammond than his need. She was certain of it.

"I would say so, what other reason could there possibly be?" He'd just taken root in her mind and, like a weed, wouldn't let go. The harder he pushed against her, the more she wanted to help him, even if it was just to be contrary.

"Do you know where we can find him?" The little town of Belle Fourche sat just within sight.

It was still early afternoon, about the same time she'd met him that very first day at the bank. "He should be at the bank, where he works." Talking to him there would not be easy and she didn't want him to be reprimanded for socializing when he should be working. "I can go inside and find out when he is finished for the day. Then we can take him back to his boarding house for coffee."

Papa laughed. "You have this all planned out? I thought I'd surprised you."

She'd been so happy about her father rising from his bed that she hadn't considered why she was completely ready for such a trip. Perhaps she was as impetuous as her father had accused. She certainly had thrown every thought, willing or not, onto the project of Cody Hammond without consultation or planning. Hopefully, he was a worthy one.

CHAPTER 15

A tall wagon, completely boxed in, caught Cody's eye as it lumbered down the street in front of the clinic where he waited for Anne to finish seeing a patient. He'd never seen the rig before and, even after only living in town a few months, he recognized most people by either their horses or the wagons they drove. He searched the marred paint for a name or clue as to who it could be, then, giving up on the puzzle, glanced at the driver and gripped his chair tightly as Natalie and an older man drove by.

He'd almost forgotten what it felt like to hop out of a chair without thinking, but he only made it a few inches before he dropped back into his seat. He couldn't just run out there and see what she was doing, because he simply couldn't move that fast. Anne came into the room, pulling his attention from outside back to the reason he'd come.

"Cody, I'm sorry to make you wait. I was hoping to visit with you during lunch, while I locked up. I have people coming in all afternoon, but I have a short break now. Bring your crutch over to the table here. I noticed at church the padding had worn down."

His underarm throbbed and he resisted telling her about it. He didn't need her touching him. Fixing the pad would fix the problem. In a few days, he'd feel fine again. He followed her to the narrow metal bed and sat on it, handing her his crutch. He hadn't really noticed how dirty and worn it looked until he had to give it to someone else to handle.

Anne gave a half-smile as she gathered cotton roving and white fabric from a cabinet along the back wall of the clinic. "I'm glad to see this. It means you've been using it. When you came to Belle Fourche, you did little but sit in that boarding house and brood your days away. I was afraid you might not get back on your feet."

His wheeled chair had been fine in London where everything was on the street, no steps to climb just to go into a store. Buildings in America, especially the West, all seemed to be built off the ground in such a way that required a boardwalk or stairs to get in. The crutches were a necessity of life.

"It was a stipulation of working for the bank. They couldn't lower the counter for me, so I had to find a way to seat myself higher. I also needed to be able to get to work." He didn't have to describe the big bank building with its stone face and one large step leading to the double doors. It could've just as well been a mountain in his wheeled chair.

"I think it's a good thing. It strengthens you." She took a scissors and cut the old pad off, leaving just a wooden T.

"You think I'm a fool, don't you?" Anne probably knew about Natalie's offer and was only trying to get him to do it. If Anne wanted him to, then the decision was made, he certainly wouldn't do it.

"Why, yes, but what instance are you referring to?" Her gray eyes, just like his own, glimmered at him.

"You think I should accept the *gift* from Natalie, to make her father happy." It was difficult not to grind out the word.

Anne frowned, then directed her gaze to her work. "I think she's a dear for wanting to help you return to a more normal life. It's very kind." Anne wound the batting around the top of the crutch.

"A dear—" He took a deep breath. "I don't like it." It made Natalie too much like Anne, and he had enough with one Anne to bother him, two would be too much.

"You don't like it? That she wants to do you a kindness?" It took a moment for her to bind the batting with a thin strip of cotton, then she set the crutch aside to sit next to him.

"I want you to know, Cody, you aren't the only one who has trouble accepting a kindness. Eli couldn't either. He didn't think he deserved it because of what he'd done. Living life without kindness is no way to live. I'd be happy to help you if you need me to listen, if there's anything you need to confess—"

He choked and his spine straightened in the seat like a rod. "Confess? *I've* done nothing and who are you to try to examine my thoughts?" She was the one who needed to confess, to apologize for needing a wayward governess, for breaking apart their family, for getting married instead of returning with him to England.

"The anger has to come from somewhere. When you're ready to tell me. I'm here." She patted his shoulder and went back to her spot by the wall, carefully wrapping the white fabric around the padding, then slowly and neatly sewing it closed. About the time she finished, the door opened, letting in a breeze. Anne glanced up, then stood.

"Natalie, what's the matter?"

Cody turned, and at the door stood Natalie with an older man draped over her arm. He was wheezing and leaning heavily against her. Cody grabbed his crutch to stand, but what could he do to help? He couldn't balance the man or take the weight off Natalie's shoulders. Anne rushed over and slid the man's arm around her own neck, taking half the weight.

"To the bed," she said quickly and both women maneuvered the man to the nearest bed, then laid him down, but the moment he was reclined, coughing claimed his breathing until he turned a deep crimson, then a terrifying gray. Cody shifted in his seat and held his own breath. He'd been caught in a situation he could not help and he didn't want to watch a man die. There had been too much of that in the army.

Anne went to the cabinet and got out a bottle with some elixir in it and a spoon. Once the man was able to take a breath between coughs, she gave him a spoonful. Though it seemed to take many minutes, the coughing subsided and he drifted to sleep.

"When did this start?" Anne took a stethoscope from a doctor's bag behind the one desk in the whole office. She placed the two ends in her ears and the cone to the man's chest.

"Father has been sick for some time."

So, this was the father that he was supposed to make happy, the man who made limbs for people like him. Castaways. Misfits. But did it really help, or just make it worse? Were they seen as even odder after the fact?

"His lungs are full of fluid." Cody had never seen Anne speak so gravely.

"He," Natalie paused, glanced back at him for a moment, her soft eyes imploring him, "He coughed up blood earlier."

Anne nodded and put the stethoscope away. "I have no way of knowing if the blood is coming from his lungs or his windpipe. Sometimes, long periods of coughing or inhaling something harsh can tear up the airway. It might not be coming from the lungs. There's no way for me to know that just by listening."

"But it won't kill him, right? He's wrong about that." Natalie's voice got higher, taking on a hysterical quality and Cody slipped the crutch under his arm to leave. He didn't know Natalie and didn't need to be there to listen to her. Especially if the talk was of private matters, like death.

"Please don't leave, Cody." Natalie stood and a moment later, her liquid-green eyes were before him. She knelt in front of him and gripped his hands. He wanted to pull away, away from her expression of sweetness and her humility at his feet. It was yet more kindness that was like a burn to his skin, yet he couldn't.

"You see what I'm up against? You see how sick he is? Please, let us do this for you. Let us help you, and in so doing, help him. He needs to remember what it's like to help people so he fights. So he gets better."

Her hands were hot against his cool skin and he slipped them off. She flinched and he decided to do the unexpected, since she was so good at surprising him. He took her hands in his own. Anne had said the limb would be a good thing, and she was right. It would help him in his job, not to become Mr. Langerford's right hand as the banker wanted, but to go back to England as *he'd* wanted.

Saving money was only half the battle. He'd saved, and almost had enough. The part he'd been unsure of was how he could survive another trip across the ocean with his crutch or chair. It had been difficult on the voyage to America. A leg would mean he could walk, go below deck without help, do everything everyone else could. He wouldn't be trapped.

Yes, it was a kindness and he didn't want to take it from her, but it was also a means to an end. England might wait forever, but he couldn't.

"You do have a way with words." He squeezed her small hands and her mouth opened just slightly in surprise and his eyes were drawn to it. Her pupils shrank to tiny dots. Everything about her suddenly came into focus—her scent, the color of her lashes, the soft curve of her cheek. He loosed her hands and let them drop.

"Does that mean you will?" From her position on the floor, the hope in her eyes worked against all the harsh anger he'd fostered for years. Her eyes had the same sweet innocent quality the abandoned dogs had that came to the back door of the boarding house. Had Natalie been thrown to the wolves as well?

"I will. What do I need to do?"

Anne clucked her tongue from next to Mr. Oleson's bed and flattened her lips. "I'll get my measuring tape."

CHAPTER 16

Natalie collected herself off the floor and went back to her father's bed. The nape of her neck prickled and she knew, without turning, that Cody followed her with his eyes. She'd just had a small victory, but her heart seemed certain she'd won the war with the way it pattered on.

"Did you hear, Papa? Anne is going to take measurements for Cody's leg. We can do it." She touched her father's shoulder, but he didn't move. Whatever Anne had given him to take away the cough had him in a deep sleep. Anne hadn't answered the question about her father's health, but perhaps that was a question for the doctor. Or one she just didn't want to have to say.

When they'd arrived in Belle Fourche, Papa had asked that they not go get the doctor, insisting that he couldn't help someone who was going to die. She'd been angry at the time, telling him that doctors were there to prevent death, but he'd been so morbid lately, his mind couldn't be turned. She still wondered if the doctor could do some good they hadn't considered.

When he'd almost fallen from the wagon because he was so weak after spending two hours riding to town, then around town looking for Cody, he'd finally agreed to let her take him to the doctor. She just prayed it wasn't too late.

Over the last few months, she'd been terrified to pray for her father, that if she brought her father's health to the Lord, that meant he was sicker than she'd let herself admit and that it meant she didn't trust the Lord's goodness. God was good, all the time, and used even the bad things for His glory. Her father would pull through this and it would bring glory to God.

With a bowed head, she wanted to pray, wanted to let out the worries nagging at her, but the words would not come. It was too much of a test of her trust.

Anne rested a hand on her shoulder. "Natalie. I have Cody's measurements here." Anne handed her a slip of paper. "Leave your father here with me. He can't go anywhere and I'd like Dr. Spight to look at him when he gets back. If the doctor thinks he can go home, I'll bring him back out to the ranch when I go home after work. Can you please take Cody back to the boarding house? It's a very long way to walk from here." Something similar to a growl came from Cody and Anne laughed. "He's all bluster, and it *is* a long walk."

Natalie found herself nodding, but she wanted to stay with her father. If he woke up all alone in a strange place, would he be worried? Would he wonder where she'd gone or that she'd abandoned him? She'd been with him almost all the time since they'd come to Belle Fourche.

Anne shoved the paper into her hand and helped her stand. "Go. Let him rest now. You should rest, too. When he gets home, you'll be back to caring for him."

Her father had never asked anything of her, she'd always just offered to help, but Anne's words brought her work into focus. She hadn't had a break in a long time and she was bone weary.

Cody stood with the aid of his crutch and flinched as the weight of his body rested over it. "Are you all right?" She gathered her thoughts and squeezed her father's hand as a goodbye.

Though he seemed to want to ignore her by glancing around the room, Cody finally answered her. "I'm fine. Just concerned about my reputation. Riding around the town with two unmarried women in one day." He slapped his hat on his head and turned for the door.

She laughed at his joke and was thankful for the bit of light it offered in an otherwise bad situation. "You'll have to tell me where the boarding house is. I don't know." She opened the door for him.

He gave her a strange look as she held the door and she gasped, realizing she'd treated him as if he were a woman, or child. "I—" What could she say to make him understand she only wanted to help, not insult? Hadn't her own father just told her she had to stop doing things without thinking?

Cody walked through the door and headed for her rig without a word, his spine rigid. She stopped, wondering how he could've known which wagon to go to. He went around the back and she rushed to help. The door was not easy to open without knowing how and he wouldn't be able to climb up into the seat.

Once she made it behind the wagon, she found him leaning against the wall, trying to work the latch.

"It sticks. Let me."

His gray eyes flicked to hers, cold, angry. "You're just opening every door for me today, aren't you?"

If Papa was right, there was a reason for his anger, something as big as the ocean that made him snap. She touched his arm and she felt his muscles twitch and recoil under her fingers. "I mean you no disrespect, Cody. I wouldn't do that." She took the heel of her hand and hit the wood just above the latch. It fell loose and she twisted it to open the door. "I'm sorry that it's not comfortable back here. We didn't go inside often, only when it was too wet to keep moving."

He sat on the floor in the doorway of the box and pushed his crutch in behind him, holding the door open. He didn't address her concern or even accept her apology. "You keep going down main to fourth, then take a right. It's the last house on the left."

She pursed her lips and went around to the front, feeling punished for her actions. Why was this man angrier than any other she'd met? The chip on his shoulder was so large it was practically visible to any onlooker, which explained why no one had wanted to help him. Cody Hammond was alone.

Within a few minutes, she stopped in front of a large home with a few people sitting out front. Cody was already out of the back by the time she climbed down and he pushed the door closed, securing it.

"Thank you. I think I can manage from here. No reason to walk me up to the doorway."

Was he teasing her, because she'd opened the last two? Or would he really rather she'd stay away from him. He was too grumpy to tell.

"Perhaps you could open the door for me?" She clutched her hands behind her back and waited for him to respond. If Cody was lonely, and she was lonely without anyone but her father, then there was no reason they couldn't keep each other company.

"Are you inviting yourself in?" He raised his brows and, though she'd seen that same look as mocking, he now appeared shocked.

"Not to your room, of course, but you could show me the boarding house. I'm not familiar with Belle Fourche, so I'd like to see more of it." She prodded without touching him.

"No one comes here to visit me. Even Anne stays away now that she's married," he mumbled and her heart melted a little more for the lonely, gruff man.

He led her up the walk, but said little as he slowly climbed the four stairs to the porch, using a method that left her holding her breath and praying he wouldn't fall. Once he reached the top, he opened the door and swung it wide. "Welcome, to my little asylum."

CHAPTER 17

Most of the men and women who lived at the boarding house weren't there during the day, leaving Cody alone with Natalie in the large sitting room. When he'd arrived in Belle Fourche he used to sit there and watch out the window, unable to do much else. Back then, he'd hated the old house and the fact that they'd needed to put him in a strange alcove on the main floor because he couldn't go up the stairs where the other sleeping quarters were. The house was full of cowboys who followed the cattle work, dusty folks who carried that blasted American swagger. Belle Fourche was booming as the county seat. Now that the railroad was running, some said the label had been stolen from a nearby town because of the intervention of Seth Bullock. The cattle stockyard provided jobs to an otherwise struggling state economy, which meant *more* cowboys.

Since he couldn't show Natalie the rooms, nor did he feel like taking her to the basement to see the kitchen and dining room, there was very little to show her. He glanced around at the various furniture pieces lined up around the room with framed photographs covering the walls. No one had ever said who they were, leaving that a topic he couldn't broach.

Natalie took a few steps toward the piano along one wall and made a small joyful gasp as her fingers played discordant notes, playfully, like a child. "A piano! Do you play?"

He hadn't thought about the piano in years, though he'd lived at the boarding house, seen the instrument in passing, for months. The notes and Natalie's voice, so excited, were just like Anne's as a young girl. The old scene played before his eyes without his permission, as if it fought for purchase.

Please, Cody, play me a song.

His fingers twitched and flexed, trying to remember. By the time Anne had been old enough to learn the piano, Father and Mother were no longer speaking, and the dreaded thing had been left tuneless. It was before the governess would take Father away, before he'd gone off to fight losing battles, before he'd lost the little happiness he'd allowed in his life. He'd forgotten that the house had been cold years before then. He'd forgotten just how cold it had been between his parents. The very reason he'd chosen to turn his love to his country, and not his family.

"I, don't remember," he muttered. His knee buckled slightly and he leaned on the crutch a moment before he would've lost his balance. "I don't want to remember." How could he have forgotten his life so completely before losing his leg? He'd been so convinced that it was Anne's fault. He stared at the instrument, wishing he could stop the flood of memories it—and Natalie—had caused.

Natalie was there in a heartbeat, sensing his infernal

weakness and wrapping an arm around him. "Let's go out back and sit." He managed through a lodged throat. He needed air. How could he have forgotten the piano?

"Cody, did I say something wrong? Are you all right?" Natalie propped him up as they walked down the narrow hall to the back of the house and out on the porch.

He couldn't answer her. He'd blamed Anne completely for the breakup of the family, but the governess had been only the last straw. Father and Mother had gone their separate ways without separating long before Cody had lost his leg. Long before the governess had even come to Hammond Place.

Natalie sat down next to him and he couldn't remember finding the chair or getting himself into it. A yellow dog he'd name Dusty approached, hunkered down with its tail hiding. He'd always felt like he and the dogs were the same, cast out by circumstance, but if that was the case, then Anne was just as lost, and he'd dashed her against even more rocks. How had he managed to find compassion for a mutt, but not his own blood?

"I'm sorry I've been so rude." He glanced at her and her soft hazel eyes caressed his face.

"Does it hurt when people bring up the past? I can only assume that's what happened, with the piano." She reached for his hand and patted it softly, like he'd done to the dog's head.

"Yes," he confirmed. Right up until the time he'd gone into the English Army he'd played songs for Anne. She'd been so young and didn't understand why her parents were unhappy. She'd clung to Cody, loved him…needed him. He'd feared leaving her there with Mother and Father, but he'd had a duty to his country. He'd had to escape his parents while he could. He'd let that duty destroy both himself and his sister, eventually.

"Why did you keep after me when I treated you so poorly?" he asked. "Most people don't bother giving me a second chance and I like my peace, so that's fine by me." At least, it had been. He wanted peace at that moment too, but not from Natalie. The memories inundated him, the snipping, the separate rooms, the middle of the night fights, the whispers of the staff, he'd known all along, yet blocked it all from his memory. He had the absurd urge to reach for her hand again and hold it like he had in Dr. Spight's office. Instead, he gripped the bench to keep his hands just where they should stay.

She smiled for just a moment, then a tear ran down her cheek and she quickly dashed it away. Her glance sank to her lap. "I guess I'm just lonely. Papa was my only real acquaintance. My brothers are fine, but after Mama died, they looked to me more like a mother than a sister. A mother they didn't have to obey." She chuckled, but it was hollow.

He took a deep breath and moved his hand just a hair closer to her on the bench. The more she spoke, the more he wanted to offer her some comfort. She'd offered to give him his freedom and had, in fact, freed him unknowingly from part of his past. He'd never felt particularly warm to the plight of others unless it was the dogs he helped, but she made him want to.

Dusty nosed his way up the stairs and laid his head in Cody's lap.

Natalie reached for the dog and Dusty growled slightly and nipped at her hand. In an instant, Cody grabbed the dog by the back of the neck and held him off. Natalie slid away from him on the bench.

"He won't hurt you, he just doesn't know you yet."

Cody released his hold on the dog and gave him a command not to bite. The dog whined and laid his head back on Cody's lap. "Go downstairs to the kitchen and ask Mrs. Turlish for the lunch scraps for Dusty. She'll give them to you."

Natalie left him and he stared at the dog. "When I'm not trying to chase her away, she is a rather sweet girl, and too pretty for her own good."

Dusty whined and nudged his knee. The dog knew that if Cody sat out there, that meant it was time to eat. He always brought scraps with him to feed to the poor dog. "What will you do when I go back to England? Who will feed you then?" He'd thought and planned and worked through every problem that could arise for the trip back to his homeland, but now it left him worried. If he'd replaced the love of his parents with England, could he just as easily change his love for England for something else? Was allegiance really that fickle?

Natalie returned and handed him a metal bowl with scraps in it. Dusty sat up and lifted a paw, waiting for him to put the bowl down. He pushed it back into her hands.

"You put it down for him, then he'll learn that you won't hurt him. His name is Dusty, and he needs someone kind. Someone to take care of him when I'm gone. Do you think the Olesons will allow a dog out there, with you?" He turned to face her and she sat staring at him, blinking rapidly.

"You're going away, too?"

CHAPTER 18

It had to be because her father was so sick. She couldn't possibly be affected by the loss of such a surly man. Natalie stared at Cody and could not figure out why her heart ached at hearing that he was leaving. She'd assumed, either because his sister was there or perhaps, selfishly, because he was infirm, that he would always be in Belle Fourche. Of all the people she'd met, though he'd been rude, he had seemed the safest. He'd been the one she could offer her friendship and never have to worry about losing. She'd faced all his barbed words based on that assessment.

"Didn't Anne tell you? We are from England, and I'd like to return there."

"But, your leg—" She stopped before she could say more. He was so prone to anger at the mere mention of it.

Instead of the gruff furrowing of his brow as she'd expected, he sighed and leaned forward, patting Dusty on the head while he ate. Now that the dog had food, he seemed as agreeable as could be. After a minute, Cody glanced back up at her. "My leg, or rather the lack, was a hardship for me coming to America. It's one of the reasons I finally gave in and agreed to the false limb."

Cody must have been stronger than she thought to have gone across the ocean with only a crutch. "I can't even fathom what it must have been like."

He shook his head and continued to pet the dog, who seemed to sense his master was straining and shifted his body closer to Cody, leaning into the attention. "Worse than you think. After my time at a *home* in England, I no longer had the strength to use the crutch. I was only allowed my chair. I couldn't catch my balance long enough to keep myself from falling on the ship, so I stayed below for the majority of the trip, mostly in my bed, using my crutch only when necessary."

Unable to stop herself, she reached over and touched his elbow. She needed the contact, the delicate intimacy of a gentle touch. He watched her hand as if he expected her to pull away, but instead, she slid her hand around his arm and just held it. "I'm sorry. I wish there was more I could do for you. I've helped my father since Mama died. I don't see helping anyone as a sign of weakness."

He ducked his head, but she hadn't meant to defeat him. "I've been such a mule, Miss Oleson. Stubborn. Rude. All because I'd forgotten a very important piece of my history. I wouldn't accept kindness from anyone, and only gave back what I was required to because manners dictated I must."

"That must have been lonely." She slid closer to him until their arms touched and as she did, she slid her hand down his arm until it was at his wrist, just above where his hand gripped the seat. She wouldn't take his hand without his permission, but sitting next to him, finally giving him the understanding he needed, warmed her after the cold reality of seeing her father return to illness so quickly.

"I don't think about it as lonely. I tend to stay in my own mind most of the time. I guess I didn't even realize what I'd turned into. I'd forgotten I wasn't always that way. I used to play with Anne at the park. I protected her from a bullish little boy in the schoolyard. I read to her. I —" his voice broke and he turned away, "played the piano for her."

He slid his hand up slightly and clasped her fingers tightly. "I'd forgotten."

"You may have forgotten, it may have been a surprise to you, but it wasn't a surprise to God." She laid her other hand over his when she felt him pulling away.

He scoffed. "God? Where was He on the battlefield? You say nothing is a surprise, you would say that this—" He stopped petting the dog and pointed to his pant leg, tied in a knot where it ended at the end of his thigh. "— is God's will?"

She held tight to him. He needed to see, to understand that God's foreknowledge and His will were two different things. "You don't know what His will is. You don't know that you weren't spared death instead."

"Battle doesn't work that way." His breathing became deeper and more pronounced and she was sure that if he could have made an easy run for the door, he would've.

"Then perhaps you saved someone's life by sacrificing a bit of yourself. You won't know until you meet God, but He is good and nothing happens outside of His understanding. All things, good and bad, work to the glory of God."

Now he furrowed his brows in anger. She'd gone too

far and her mind told her to recoil while her heart told her to hang on with all she had.

"And if He takes your father home, is that His good will?"

She released his hand and her heart went cold. She stood, ready to escape. He'd spoken aloud her worst fear and she couldn't agree with it. "He wouldn't," she whispered.

"So, it's all right—it's within His will—to take my leg, but not your father?"

She couldn't answer that, didn't want to. Couldn't admit he might be right. What did he know? He had no faith. He hadn't heard Mama talk about God. Natalie spun quickly from him and went back inside and through the boarding house, back out to her wagon and climbed to the seat. Her tears wouldn't help her drive, but she needed to get away from him.

Once she had wiped her tears and slid on her leather driving gloves, she gathered the lines and stared ahead. Something about Cody, whether he was being nice as a Sunday dinner or as cold as winter, hit her more deeply than anyone else. It was as if, just by speaking, he'd burrowed his way to the special place in her heart reserved for those whose esteem mattered. Cody mattered. That's why his barbed words, and his confessions, affected her so.

She glanced back at the house and the curtain in the window fluttered back closed. Someone had watched her sitting there, and there hadn't been anyone in the house when she'd walked through, so it had to have been Cody. How could he still care enough to follow her after cruelly tearing down what she believed?

Could he be right? Could it be God's will to take her father home soon? What of her and her brothers? God couldn't take him and still care about her and her brothers, could He? She flicked the lines and guided the horses back to the road that would take her to the ranch. With all the people who lived on the ranch, she could surely find someone to talk to about her fears. Because she wasn't ready to let go.

CHAPTER 19

Someone knocked on the door jamb as Cody sat out behind the boarding house. He'd returned to his spot after watching Natalie, to make certain she made it to her rig. She'd been so hurt and flummoxed by his words that he'd been worried about her. Was still worried about her. Worse, her words had made him think.

He'd had faith when he was young. He'd let go of what little was left of it the moment they took his leg, as if they'd amputated part of his soul right along with his knee. Faith hadn't saved his career. He'd planned to serve his country his whole life.

Anne sat on the bench where Natalie had been. It was now later in the evening. Supper had probably passed, he couldn't remember and hadn't gone down to eat.

"I came by to make certain Natalie wasn't still here. Dr. Spight would rather her father not leave the clinic for a while."

Though he didn't mean to, Cody flinched. Natalie

would take it hard. "Are you going to tell her?" Would his words make the blow even harder? Would she think of death when Anne was only bringing news of illness, because of him?

"Yes. I'll stop at the house on my way home and let her know. I expect she'll want to ride with me in the morning. Perhaps when you're done with your day at the bank, you could come down to see her, make sure she gets out of that clinic for a few minutes. She'll want to sit right next to that bed, but it won't change the outcome. The doctor thinks that perhaps years of inhaling the finish for the wooden limbs has hurt his lungs, irreparably. But there's just no way to know for certain."

He nodded, but didn't care. The *why* didn't matter, only that it would happen. "You're sure? He is terminal?"

She bowed her head, her face tense and tired. "Yes. He may get temporarily better with the medication, but it's only a matter of time. Once he is well enough to move, we'll bring him back home for his last days."

"This will break her," he muttered, unable to hold it in. For so long he'd cared about so few that Natalie's pain ate at him. She had no one in this world. Even *he* had the dog and he didn't even deserve that. Not after how he'd been.

"And you care?" Anne raised an eyebrow and met his gaze.

"I do. I don't know why, but I do." He reached for her hand, as he should've done with Natalie, and took it in his own. "I'm sorry. I apologized to Natalie earlier, but I owe you more. I've been horrible. She didn't mean to, but she reminded me today that our parents were apart before your governess tore them completely. I blamed you. She was *your* governess. If you hadn't needed her—"

He stopped. Any more and it would be an accusation. Anne had to hurt about the separation just as much as he did, but she had to understand why he'd held onto his pain so long.

"When they sent me away, I tried to escape so many times. They took my crutches away and strapped me into my chair. It's pretty hard to move when you're in a wheeled chair without the use of your arms." He lifted his hands out in front of him, his sleeves moving up slightly to reveal the light scarring from trying to loosen the wide leather straps and the deep purple wavy one from his burn on his hand.

Anne's mouth dropped open and her eyes turned glassy. "I didn't know."

"No one did. Mother and Father didn't come to visit, you had been sent to live with Uncle Sydney. I only knew that because I begged them to know what happened to you and they taunted me with it."

She shook her head as a tear escaped the guard of her lashes and she didn't bother to wipe it away. "They never told me where you went. I didn't know until you came here and told me. I thought you'd gotten to stay with Mother or Father. No one ever told me where you were. You'd been locked away so long before that. After your anger—"

There was no other way to describe what he'd done. He'd been furious over the loss of his leg, his inability to do anything. He'd been furious with Anne for trying to help him, for being whole, and he'd goaded her into joining the army. He'd pushed her into doing something she may never have done, just for the love of a brother who couldn't give any at the time. She'd loved him in place of her parents, and he'd used it.

"I can never make up for what I've done to you,

Anne. It's all so clear to me now. One little phrase from the past and it all came flooding back as if it had been locked behind a door. And after helping me break through, I was horrible to Natalie again."

Anne patted his hand, the warmth new to him. "You are welcome to come with me to talk to her tonight. It may help soften what I have to say."

He laughed. "When has anything that I've said ever softened anyone?"

She wiped another tear from her cheek. "I think you might be surprised. I think Natalie sees more in you than even you do. She's been asking everyone about you since she arrived. We all thought it was just to get information about your leg, but maybe there's more to it."

He recalled the look of hurt in her eyes when he said he'd planned to go back to England, and how empty the statement had been, even to him. "I should go and talk to her, but it's late and I must work tomorrow. I don't think I can go with you all the way out there, talk to her, and ride all the way back."

"You can stay with Nathan and Maretta at the house, then come back with me in the morning. We'd be happy to have you."

He sat for a moment and thought about it. He wouldn't be able to sleep until he found a way to take back what he'd said to Natalie. Even if he believed what he said, he'd said it in a way to hurt her, to make her give up her own faith and see it as foolish. He'd been the man he realized he hated, and that had to change.

"I'll get my coat and hat."

Anne laughed and patted his hand again then stood. "I'll be waiting out front."

CHAPTER 20

Papa wasn't home to help her with the start of the prosthetic, which was the most difficult part, but Natalie needed to do something to force her mind off of Cody's words. She sat out on the sunny porch with her paper and the measurements Anne had given her. She'd made a sketch of what the leg would have to look like, the wooden cage she would have to make, and how much leather and strapping she would need.

Many companies now made prosthetic devices, but they were expensive and some were heavy and difficult to use. Most of the *missing men* she'd spoken to had tried the devices and found their crutches to be better, until they'd tried one made by her father. He'd shown her how to make a wooden frame that was strong, yet light. He'd shown her how to build it, fasten it, seal it, and stretch the leather over it so that it looked and acted as much like a real leg as was possible. They even fashioned feet, so that the wearer could put on boots like any other man.

A hint of dust in the distance caught her eye and she put down her chisel and watched it. Anne would be coming home soon, Eli had stopped by and mentioned she was even later than usual. If she was bringing Father with her, it would take her extra time and she wouldn't be able to work on the prosthesis. Anne had warned her Father might have to stay at the clinic, but he was stronger than Anne thought. He wouldn't need to. Natalie had already made sure his room was ready for him.

When the light, two-seat rig rolled up in front of the house, it was not the hunched figure of her father in the seat with Anne, but Cody. She hadn't expected to see him, not after he'd challenged her very beliefs just hours before. She'd almost allowed her anger to keep her from working toward her father's project, but that would serve to hurt her father, not Cody. He only wanted the limb so he could leave her.

Anne waited for him to climb down, but he was surprisingly capable, and part of Natalie marveled at his abilities. His arms were strong and sure, but as she watched him, there was something different about him. He had a calm she'd never noticed before.

Anne came over and rested her hand on Natalie's shoulder. "I'll be inside for a bit and I'll talk to you about your father after. Cody wanted to come out and speak to you first."

It would be rude to run and even more to stay and have the fight with him that would surely turn her heart sour toward him. Even though he'd treated her so abnormally since meeting her, she couldn't deny that he intrigued her like no one else ever had. She set aside her notes and sketches, flipping them over so he couldn't see them, and waited for Cody to come up the steps.

He sat next to her and took a deep breath. She waited for a moment, brushing the shavings of wood from her lap, then remembered her manners. "Good evening." Though without her father home, and staring down the barrel of a fight, the evening didn't feel good in the slightest.

"Is it?" Cody turned to face her. "I guess I've got nowhere to start but directly. I had no right to question your faith earlier. Of course death is worse than losing a limb. I shouldn't have compared the two."

Cody's words caught her unawares. He'd had a revelation and given her an apology earlier, but she wasn't expecting it to happen again. "I'm not so sure. I doubt the one who is dead, especially if he is with Christ, would agree. It isn't as if he is suffering anymore. What I question is how a just God," she paused, praying she got her thoughts and words correct. "A good God, could take my father from me when I've already lost so much?" She glanced at him and he didn't look down on her, nor did his face turn stony as she'd expected.

"I've had no faith for a long time, but I seem to recall that even David, who went through some distressing things, did not lose his belief that God was good."

She flinched. Had he changed his thinking because of her, or was he simply saying words to placate her? "You didn't feel that way a few hours ago. You blamed God for taking your leg."

He leaned back in his seat and she took a moment to appreciate his profile. He had dark hair, neatly trimmed, and a fine nose. She liked the way his cheek sloped, then angled down to his lips. Her favorite feature, however, was how his shoulders, broad from carrying his weight, were just the perfect breadth to carry burdens like those on her heart.

"You gave me something to think about, and I did, deeply." His lips pursed slightly. "I sat in that chair without moving, talking through my thoughts with Dusty. He didn't have much to add."

She chuckled, unable to stop herself. "Truly? He seemed so enlightened." Talking to him made the worry about her father, and why he hadn't come back with Anne, lessen just a bit.

Cody reached for her hand. "May I? I seem to think better when I'm holding your hand."

She remembered earlier when his callused fingers had encapsulated her own rough ones and she reached out to him. He smiled and took it, resting it loosely on the seat between them.

"He's a good listener. I tend to work through problems on my own, thinking of every option and every circumstance, then I put them in lists, to help me see everything more clearly. It's how I escaped the home where I lived before, and how I made it all the way to America."

He'd had to escape his home? What kind of place could he have lived that he'd had to formulate a plan to get away? "Why do you want to return somewhere you escaped from?"

He flinched and she felt it through his hand.

"We'll discuss that later, it's not the reason I came all the way out here. You were right that a good God wouldn't take a man's leg or a daughter's father, but those things still happen. So, we must come to the logical conclusion that either there is no God, or our definition of good is faulty."

She couldn't let go of her God. Even when Cody had tested her thinking, she'd been more willing to give up her reasoning than she was to give up her faith completely. "Admitting my mother may have been wrong hurts terribly. She is the one who explained it to me."

He leaned closer to her. "And how old were you when she explained it?"

Natalie rested in the healing warmth of his nearness and gentle speech, gentleness that had been so rare for him before. "Perhaps ten. Old enough to understand."

"Ten is old enough to understand, but not old enough to practice. At ten, you are still able to look at even hard things in life with a cheery countenance because most haven't known true hardship yet. I would wager it was quite easy to see God as good when your belly was full, your parents were alive, and you were happy."

That was true, though even when her mother had died, she'd convinced herself it had happened within the goodness of God. It was only when He might take her father also that she'd questioned it. "Yes, but my father cannot leave."

Cody slid a little closer to her. "I can't say what the Lord has planned for you. Perhaps someone is right here in Belle Fourche, ready to take care of you and love you, maybe even better than your father. You can't know that. None of us can see what the future holds. No matter how much I think or try. You confounded me, Natalie. I'm always able to figure out what people will do, so I can always answer the correct way, and always be one step ahead. But not with you. I couldn't figure out why. How did you continue to do things for me that I didn't deserve? How could you react in unexpected ways? It was because of your faith. I didn't take it into account."

She hadn't considered that there would ever be

someone for her. At twenty-eight, she was past her prime, though she'd been told there were many men in Belle Fourche. The prospect of meeting one was daunting. "Do you truly believe someone will care for me and that I won't be alone? Do you believe the Lord has provided for me even before my need arises?"

A brief smile touched his lips and her heart raced at it. Was he giving her a hint? Was *he* the man he meant?

"I can't know that. But I do know that you'll need to be prepared. Anne told me that your father is gravely ill. He will never fully recover. She wanted to tell you, but I feel close to you right now, and felt it best to tell you myself."

She tried to pull away from him, to run off and hide the tears she felt burning their way rapidly through her, but he tugged her close instead and pulled her against his shoulder. She couldn't hold it back and sobbed into him. His arm went around her and held her, his strength shouldn't have been surprising, but it was. He held her close and let her cry, his tenderness almost as shocking as the news.

"How?" she gasped into his shoulder. It simply wasn't fair, she couldn't accept it.

"His lungs have been damaged, but there's no way of knowing for sure why." She heard his words through his chest and she clutched his jacket as another wave of grief crashed over her.

"I had to be the one to tell you. I couldn't ask my sister to, when you might hate her for it. Better that you hate me."

But she couldn't. Not after his gruff behavior, not after questioning her faith, not even after bringing the news of her father, she could not hate him. She pulled back and searched his face. He had come to mind often over the last few days, getting more handsome and desirable by the day, and especially so on this day when he'd shown her who he'd once been and who he wanted to be again.

"I don't hate you, Cody. I'm not so sure I could."

CHAPTER 21

Cody leaned into Natalie, sure he hadn't heard her correctly. She smiled at him and rested her cheek against his shoulder once again as her sobs slowly subsided. She had to have said it, but could he believe it? He'd done so much to earn her dislike, yet she clung to him.

He'd been certain since he'd lost his leg that no woman would ever desire his company and he'd done his best to fulfill his own prophecy. Yet, the most beautiful woman he'd ever seen was now in his arms? If God was looking down on him at that moment, then grace had to be real, because he didn't deserve what he'd gotten. It was a gift in the truest sense.

She sighed slightly and leaned away from him. "I'm sorry for dampening your shoulder." Her cheeks tinged with pretty color, even in the fading light.

"It will dry. Are you all right?" He pulled his handkerchief from his pocket and handed it to her, ashamed he hadn't thought to have it out before he'd told her.

She took it and wiped her tears, then clutched it in

her lap. "Yes, perhaps. I don't think I can really prepare for it. I don't think I'll ever be ready, but at least I know."

"Anne told me he would be able to come home soon. Anne will take you in to see him tomorrow."

"Are you staying out here at the ranch tonight, then?"

He wanted to, but it would mean he would have to stay with Nathan and Maretta, in the same house as Natalie. He already didn't want to let her go this evening, would in fact have loved to recline with her in the swing where they sat and just rest in each other's arms, but that was wishful thinking.

"I don't know. I know Anne is too tired to take me back tonight," he replied.

"We'd be glad to take you back. Especially if you don't move away from my sister." A man's voice came from beyond the porch.

"George!" Natalie pulled back away from him farther. "Don't be rude to a guest."

The moment was lost. The space between them seemed to grow by the moment. George swaggered up to the steps and stood there, staring at him.

"You the one she's going to make the limb for?" George's toothpick bobbed with each word.

Cody tensed with anticipation. George was a cowboy in every sense of the word and he hated that this man was a rugged version of a man, something he could never be again. If George continued to point out his faults, then Cody would have to fight him. Though he wouldn't win. "I am, though that isn't my reason for coming."

"I can see why you came. You stay away from her. She's not fit to see you or anyone else right now."

"I don't see that it's any of your concern. You're not

her father, nor do you give her the respect she's due." Cody growled, wanting Natalie to know he was capable of holding his own.

"Respect? She doesn't need respect, she's just a bossy sister," George balked.

Cody felt Natalie collapse against him a little at her brother's cutting words.

"George," she gasped his name. "You listen to me. I won't stand for this. You won't treat me this way."

He took one menacing step up. "Listen to you? You aren't my ma, never were. If you don't see what's going on, then you got no right to make orders. He's taking advantage of your sadness over Pa's sickness. He don't even like you. He don't like anyone."

Natalie slid farther down the bench and, though he hadn't resorted to fisticuffs since he'd lost his leg, Cody now wanted to punch some sense into that fool brother of hers.

"I am not taking advantage of anyone. I came out here to give Natalie, in fact all of you, some bad news."

"Aw, shucks, that's right kind of you. You going to let me lean on you and cry on your shoulder too?" George snickered.

"George Oleson!"

Maretta came out of the house with a flour-covered rolling pin. The screened door slammed behind her and she slapped the pin against her hand. "Now, see here young man. We do not allow talk like that in my house. If you want to poke fun and be rude, do it somewhere else, but not on my property. You hear?"

He descended back down one step and the sneer slipped off his face. "Yes, ma'am."

"I thought so. Now, if you've got nothing nice to say, you git yourself back to work."

He turned and went back the way he came and Maretta regarded the two of them as she dropped her arms to her sides. "Good to see you again, Mr. Hammond."

He nodded and tried to smile, even though it stung his pride to have been protected by an older woman in front of Natalie.

"I'm sure you could've handled that boy," Maretta said, as if reading his thoughts. "But I promised Natalie that I would bring them down a peg. They need it. Conrad is working them hard as well. Soon, you'll see, they'll be respectable men."

Natalie smiled softly. "Thank you, Aunt Maretta."

The older woman retreated back into the house, but the moment was gone. He wanted to pull Natalie back into his arms, assure her that he was a man who could protect her from bullies and life, and loss, just as well as anyone else, but maybe that was false hope.

She glanced at him. "It's getting late. I should go in and talk to Anne. She will want to go home to see Eli soon."

Anne was happily married and she'd survived the same parenting he had. She'd watched their parent's marriage fall away and still managed to find love. Could he do the same? Could he convince himself he was worth it and, even more, make himself act the responsible man he needed to be?

"If I am to stay, I should go in with you and find out where I am to sleep. Perhaps the bunkhouse." Though he didn't want to be down there. He'd never gotten along well with the cowboys and especially not Natalie's brothers who treated her so poorly.

"I'd worry less if you were here in the house. There are so many rooms, I'm sure Maretta would be happy to find you a place. I'll go in and ask." She stood and he watched as she paused for a moment to glance back at him. Her soft cheeks were rounded and her eyes bright. He wasn't sure when his mind had shifted to her, perhaps it had from the moment they'd met and it had been so subtle, so secret, he hadn't noticed until he was engulfed. She pushed through the door and he was left on the porch, his skin still hot from thinking about her.

CHAPTER 22

After two days of waiting, Natalie helped move her father home. She'd hoped to see Cody while she'd been in town, but it was during the day and he'd been at the bank, working. He had stayed at the ranch that night when he'd come to tell her about her father, then ridden back to town with her and Anne the next morning, and she hadn't seen him since.

She'd managed to finish the plan for Cody's prosthesis, and she'd chiseled the wood down to thick strips that her father would then scrape down even more and put a varnish on that would help them keep their strength. Once the frame was built, they would stretch the leather over it like a skin, and attach the various fasteners to it. It took almost two weeks to complete one with just the two of them, but it would be a work of art when finished.

Father said very little to her as they rode back and even less once they had him up to his room and settled. She made herself comfortable in her chair near his bed and brought all of the pieces needed to work on Cody's leg. By having it there, she hoped it would pique her father's interest and he would want to join her. She set to work and he laid in bed, watching her.

"I know what you're up to," he told her after a few minutes. "I'm sorry, my girl, it won't work this time."

She sighed and set down the wooden dowels, then gave him her attention. "Don't you want to see my plans, see the work I've done so far, tell me where I need to improve?"

He shook his head and, though she'd hoped to, it didn't even bring a smile to his face. "No, I don't. I'm tired, Natalie. I don't have much longer."

He couldn't talk about that, not right now when she was still so raw. She would cry and it would make her father feel guilty. Even if she hated that he was leaving her, she refused to make him feel guilty for it. "I know, Father, all the more reason to work with me one last time. Please? For me?"

He sighed and held out his hands for her work. She stood and brought the notes and measurements to him. He was so weak, he couldn't even hold them up to give them a close inspection. Instead, he laid them out on the bed over his legs and glanced over them.

"You'll need to figure out another way to secure it. If you leave the stabilization strips like that, you'll cut into his hip. Put it here instead." He took up a pencil and drew a new set of straps that crossed over the hips and around him like a belt.

"And that will be comfortable?" She'd worried that it would be too heavy and it would be better over the shoulders, to provide more support.

"If you do it that way, every time he steps it will tug on his shoulders, hunching him and the connection strap will cut into his thigh."

She hadn't thought of that. Her father's designs had

always been better. Even if he'd agreed she could continue without him, she had never managed to do one all on her own. He touched her arm and pointed to the foot on the drawing.

"You've done a good job there, just make sure it's the same size as his other. Get his boot if you can, get the wood damp so it will conform to the shape."

"I had his sister measure. That part should be fine." She'd so wanted him to be impressed with her work.

"The time of people making these devices on their own is coming to a close. More and more companies are growing who can do it faster and better than those of us who do it this way. It is good that you stop now."

He didn't understand that letting go of the work they'd done together meant letting go of *him*. It meant abandoning a past she loved. Though she trusted what Cody had said, there was no fruit yet. He hadn't come to see her, and there was no one else. No one but her uncle and aunt to take care of her, and they had their hands full with their own children and grandchildren, not to mention her brothers.

"Cody came to visit two days ago. He defended me when George tried to insult me."

Her father gathered the papers and handed them back to her. "Is that so? I thought you didn't like him much, didn't trust him."

"He's changed a lot in the last few days. I'm glad to be doing this for him." She felt her cheeks burn hot. The prosthetic was a perfect excuse to see more of Cody Hammond.

"Is that so? And are you glad because he defended you, or glad because it's the right thing to do?"

She'd all but forgotten that aspect. Though she knew Cody would use the leg, it had become more of a means for both of them to speak, than for his true good. He got along fine without it. "I'm happy because I enjoy speaking to him, and I know it is the right thing."

"You've never had anyone to defend you except me. Is he taking my place already?" Father laughed, but she couldn't join him. What he said was too close to what Cody had said just a few days before.

"I don't know what you mean. He certainly isn't looking to take your place. That would be silly."

He nodded and leaned back, then slid himself down carefully into the bed. "Yes, it would be. I don't think he's looking to be a father figure to you. One who gets to you so easily, right down to making you blush… I wish I'd gotten the chance to really meet him."

Her heart ached at the thought that he might not get to if Cody didn't come back out to visit. "I'll try to make that happen," she whispered as he closed his eyes.

"You do that. I want to know that my girl will be taken care of."

"But father, it isn't like that at all." She couldn't have him believing a lie. Cody was leaving, going back to England and only leaving her a dog to care for.

He smiled softly as he drifted to sleep.

CHAPTER 23

Natalie moved all her notes, tools, and pieces back out to the front porch. The work of building a limb was messy and as much as she wanted her father to help her, she didn't want Maretta to have to worry about cleaning up a mess. Once she got everything where she wanted it on the front step, Barton ambled up, a smile on his face.

"Afternoon." Though she knew Barton to be one of the brothers who was easy to get along with, she hadn't talked to him all that much. He was quite busy with the ranch, his wife, and their twins, a boy and a girl.

"How do you do?" she answered out of habit.

"I do a lot of things, but mostly I notice things." He stopped talking to give her a brief smile that was so much like George she paused to stare for a moment. "I noticed that you haven't taken a moment for yourself since you got here. Come, take a walk with me. I'll show you around."

Everyone else was busy and her father was resting, he wouldn't need her nearby. She glanced over her shoulder, then down at her work. That too, could wait for a little while. "I would think I could take a short walk, but I must come back soon. I need to get this done. I may not have much time." She wanted her father to be able to check his changes to her design while he was still well enough to give her guidance. She would be able to watch the durability of this prosthetic more than any other, because for as long as Cody stayed, he would use it.

"Well, I'm sure I can give you the quick tour, though, there is a lot to see." He waited at the foot of the steps and she came down to meet him there. "Do you want to grab a bonnet? Sun's pretty hot."

She'd never bothered much with bonnets. Her mother hadn't forced her to do it as a young girl and she'd never gotten in the habit once her mother was gone. "I would rather go." She had no idea if he would saddle up a horse for her or just walk. The ranch was huge, but she'd never ridden a horse before. Their horses had been strictly for pulling.

"Come with me. I'll get a horse saddled for you and it won't take long. Then you'll know where everything is if you need it, or where everyone is if you need them."

It dawned on her that he wanted her to know where her brothers were, without riding out to simply watch them. "Thank you. It will be a comfort knowing where to find everyone."

"Ma can ride a horse or drive a team if she has to, in case you need the doctor, but might be easier just to round up one of us, since you'll know where we are."

She promised herself to remember everything Barton told her. She might need it soon. Her father had seemed fine, just tired, but there was no telling how long he would last.

Barton saddled a horse, then led it out to one that

waited for them outside. His horse had a white star on its forelock, hers was black with white legs. "Her name is Mule, don't laugh, I didn't name her. She was Isabelle's horse before she ever came to the ranch. She's mild for a new rider."

She turned to stare at him. "How did you know?"

He laughed. "You had a look about you, like you wanted to run when I suggested riding. We have a few horses around here that aren't fit to ride. It's Eli's job to break them and he's good at it. He'll help you find a mount if he's here. Let him be when he's out in the west pasture, though, that means he's working. If he's just working the land, he rides out to the northeast, in fact, all of us do. We left your brothers to watch over the western pastures and they're doing a good job."

"Is that where you want to start the tour?" she asked, since that was probably what he wanted to show her the most.

"Seems like a good place to start." He waited for her to mount, then clicked his tongue. He was right about Mule, she just followed Barton's horse without having to give her any direction.

When they'd ridden for what felt like quite some time, three riders appeared in the distance. They didn't notice Barton and Natalie and Barton didn't yell to distract them.

"What do they do out here?" She didn't even see any cattle nearby.

Barton pointed farther west. "They can see the fence line from there. They were told to go out and make sure none of the posts needed to be replaced and that the wires were still good. Looks like they're doing their job. They also make sure there's no problem with any cattle out here, though most have wandered down farther from the house. We can't keep a good eye on them there and we'll round them back up in the fall."

She hung her head. How had the Oleson family succeeded where she'd failed? How had they managed to turn her brothers responsible, when she'd tried her best and been unable to make them mind. They still didn't listen to her.

"I don't understand. They haven't followed a single thing I've said without having Papa make them do it. You point where to go, and they go."

Barton took his hat off and wiped his forehead with his bandanna. "Not so. Those boys are still boys, but they're learning fast, especially John. They just needed jobs, responsibility, ownership. Conrad talked to all of us and, even though it means cutting all of our shares, we decided to offer your brothers portions of the land. Sometimes, a man just has to own something for it to matter."

"Perhaps." She let it go. They weren't her trouble anymore. Now that they were in Belle Fourche to stay, they had to be men on their own or risk their standing on Oleson Ranch. "Why don't we move on?"

They turned and rode back the way they came for a while, then cut north. In the pasture, in the branches of a tall cottonwood, was a small house, the likes of which she'd never seen before. She tugged on the reins and Mule came to a stop. "Barton? What's that?" She pointed to the small dwelling in the tree.

"It's a treehouse. Pa built it for us when we were children so that we could be out here watching the cattle from high up. We'd ride out here on horse, then play up there. I haven't stopped to look at it in years. Maybe I'll bring the twins out when they're old enough."

There were slats nailed into the tree as a ladder and a

hole in the floor to climb in. The walls were complete and she could see two windows, though they looked boarded up. "Who covered the windows?"

He scratched his head. "You can take off the covers from inside. Pa designed it so that it wouldn't get wet inside in the rain, that way it won't rot the floor. I don't know if it's safe though. Let's keep going so I can get you back like you asked."

Natalie agreed. As interesting as a fort in the tree was, she couldn't stay out and investigate it. She had to be there if her father needed her.

Barton led her farther north until they reached her other three cousins, Conrad, Arnold, and Eli. They were on horseback, waiting for something. She stared all around until Eli drew his rifle, before she could shriek or understand what he would do, a shot screamed in her ears.

"Did you get it?" Arnold asked, standing in the stirrups.

"Nope. I think that was the wolf that got me. It was huge. Never seen a wolf that travels alone, but this one does." He rubbed his shoulder, but oddly not the one he'd braced the rifle against.

Natalie understood there was more to what was being said and that everyone else understood, but she didn't want to stay. "I think I'll ride back," she offered.

Eli turned and frowned. "I'm sorry, Natalie. I didn't see you there. I wouldn't have taken the shot if I'd known." His eyes were apologetic, and she appreciated that. Not having grown up on a ranch, she didn't understand why a lone wolf would be such a bother.

Barton frowned slightly. "We don't normally worry over the wolves. They stay in their packs and are mostly terrified to go near us. That one isn't. It took a hunk out of Eli's shoulder last spring and has taken two calves since. We've chased it, but it just keeps coming back."

Eli slid the rifle back in its long scabbard. Barton turned somber eyes on her and nodded his head back toward the ranch. She followed without a word.

CHAPTER 24

He'd come to think of the asylum as his prison when he'd lived there and, at his worst moments, feared he would never escape. Putting ideas on paper had always helped him control them, understand them. But not today.

The drawing didn't quite capture Cody's memory of Breckenham's Asylum for the Needy. The more lines he added, the darker the page became and the more real it seemed to him, though he'd only gotten two glimpses of the building from as far away as the perspective of his drawing.

In the back corner of the rendition, almost unnoticeable, sat a small shed. It was the very shed he'd lit ablaze as a distraction to make his escape. His hand flexed, the old scar pulled, and he squeezed the pencil until he felt it bow, but he did not break it. So long ago, but not long enough. He could still smell the smoke from the old damp rags in the back of that shed. He could smell the hay in the field that surrounded the encampment where he'd hidden until nightfall, then crawled to town and used the money from his parent's account to buy a new crutch and passage to America.

A man who had survived a London military hospital had brought word of his sister, and that she'd left for the States. He'd had purpose then and had used every ounce of it to find her.

He felt gentle pressure on his shoulder and he turned as Anne sat next to him.

"I thought I'd stop in and see you."

Odd, she'd never done that. He smiled slightly. His demeanor had changed while talking to Natalie, which made his day pass more quickly and pleasantly. But by the time he'd reached the boarding house, a dark cloud had taken over his thoughts. He'd started writing and then he'd sketched and finally it had become the drawing laying before him.

"What is it?" Anne tilted her head to get a closer look.

He laid the pencil down and slid the paper a few inches away, to separate himself from it once again. "It's nothing."

"That's where you lived, isn't it, the asylum?"

He'd told her roughly how he'd made his escape, but never details. He didn't want to revisit that day and his sister wouldn't want to hear about it. "It is, but that is in the past, best left there."

"If you're drawing it, then it was on your mind. If you need to talk, I'm here. I served in a military hospital." Her gray eyes misted. "It couldn't have been much worse."

He tried to control the anger that he'd vowed to leave behind him. Though he now knew it wasn't Anne's fault he'd been there, he didn't want to talk about it and she needed to leave well-enough alone. "After living in both, I would beg to differ."

At the asylum, people who couldn't move were left to rot on beds in their own filth. The nausea from the smell never really went away. Some of the caretakers were violent, most were unwilling to do the work that needed to get done for the pay that they got. After trying to escape, he'd been marked as trouble and the more aggressive ones seemed to watch him.

"You told me what you did to get free. I don't blame you, but perhaps," Anne frowned for a moment, "you might feel a touch of remorse."

"Remorse?" His anger exploded once again as if he'd never checked it in the first place. "I feel no such thing. What those animals did to me, daily, was atrocious. I would set fire to every building there, including the hospital itself, if it meant I could be free."

She touched his arm and waited a moment. "I don't think you mean that. There had to be people there even more infirm than you and you would've cost them their lives."

He slammed his hand down on the table, then pushed his chair back so he could walk away if she said more. "Most of them begged daily to die, Anne. I had no other options. That place is the very reason that I map out every move and every response I make. Everything must be planned until I understand every outcome, because if I don't, I control nothing. When you come from a place where you wish to die, you never want a surprise ever again."

Anne's calm features did not waver. "Even if they begged to die, you would have no right to do that for them. I wish I'd known where you were. Our uncle wouldn't tell me. He said you didn't want to hear from me, especially with my plans to leave England. He made it sound as if he was in contact with you and you were angry with me."

Though his heart still pounded, he unclenched his fist and rested his hand over Anne's. "I never said any such thing."

A tear rolled down her cheek. "I wanted to take you with me, but no one would tell me where you were. I thought perhaps you were with Father, but I had no way to know."

"See, just as I said, I had no options. You couldn't come to get me. Uncle Sydney refused to answer my letters. I didn't know where Mother or Father were, nor if they cared. I had tried to escape before and failed. I had to get free."

"I understand. What I don't understand is how you got hold of your money to come here. You said you couldn't work." She picked up the pencil and continued where he'd left off, filling in the bricks. Though she'd apparently never witnessed the building, it was a pattern easily seen.

He had used a financial loophole, and a bit of lying, to get his money. However, it was his and the asylum had no right to it if he wasn't being *cared* for there any longer. "Let's just say the Belle Fourche bank isn't the first one I've worked in, but it is the first for pay."

She sighed and set the pencil down. "I came over to talk to you because I'm worried. Natalie is not prepared to lose her father and, while I can't make any definite predictions, I know he will not last long. She seems to be closest to you. When her father passes, perhaps you could speak to Mr. Langerford and stay out at the ranch for her. She might need someone to be there. Her brothers certainly won't."

Natalie had never asked for pay for the leg she was making, but he wanted to do something for her. He'd wanted to find some reason to see her, but had come up with nothing that was a plausible reason, besides just wanting to see her and hear her voice.

"If you think that would be wise, I will talk to him." Talk of Natalie brought up another problem he'd been mulling over. "Anne, do you know of any home builders in Belle Fourche?" There was the lumberyard, but they had many jobs and their labor came at a high cost. Cody still had some of the funds from his escape, but even with his savings from the bank, it wasn't enough to pay to have his house built at extravagant cost. If he was staying, he could use the money for building.

"There just happen to be five men who consider you family, Cody. My husband, his brothers, and his father. You only have to ask." Anne raised her dark eyebrows and stood to leave. "Are you thinking about a house? I thought you were saving your money to go back to England?"

He had been. He'd clutched every penny and put it in savings. But after meeting Natalie, England didn't sound quite as much like home. They would each be alone on separate continents. He'd held it against his sister for choosing a husband over her homeland, but in the span of a little over a week, his eyes had been opened to the difficulty of making such a choice. "I didn't say I was planning anything. Simply looking into it." He wasn't quite ready to admit he wanted to stay, not until he'd really talked to Natalie outside of the grief she would have to go through. After that, he would make a decision. A permanent one.

CHAPTER 25

The sun peeked in Natalie's window and she threw off her covers, eager to get every minute with her father she could. He'd been helping with the whittling as much as he was able, but it frustrated him and he seemed to want to move from task to task quickly.

As she put on her dress for the day, she considered her father's words from the day before, "No one is making limbs this way anymore, Natalie. This way is going by the wayside. War isn't a good thing, but the War Between the States caused so many men to come home with pieces missing that there was a great need for better devices. I've always said ours were the best, but I think it's time we let the companies do it."

He'd waited for her response, because she'd never given him the promise he was looking for that she would stop once he was gone. How could she? Without a husband, she would have to find a way to earn her bread and a place to live.

"I need your word, my girl." He set down his tool and the wood and regarded her.

There was no way around his request this time. He'd probably done that on purpose. They were half done with the leg now, and would need to stretch the leather soon, which she would have to do outside. It would mean she couldn't be with him. "What will I do?"

"The Lord knows your need even before you ask it. I'm asking you to let this go. The doctor thinks it may be the varnish we use on the wood or the tanning solution that has hurt my lungs. I need your word."

She flinched. That would be it. Her word was her bond and if she did, she would have to keep it. "I will leave this behind, as you ask."

He smiled and picked up his tools once more. "I think I'll have this done by the end of the day."

Natalie blinked away the memory and finished buttoning her dress as she glanced at herself in the mirror. She quickly braided her hair, rushing so she could spend every possible minute with him. Father had worked as long as he was able the night before and he had finished tacking together the frame. She would have to secure it more firmly and then put on the varnish later, but first, she had to check on him.

Though the hall had no windows, all of the rooms had been opened so the sun could reach the hall, giving it a cheery look as she made her way to her father's room. His was the only dark patch, the only closed door. A crow called from somewhere outside, disturbing the pleasantness.

Natalie pushed open the door and her father was still sleeping, though he usually snored. Today he was silent. She crept closer to the bed to check for fever and his face was cold and stiff. Natalie yanked back her hand

and gasped. There was no rise or fall beneath the blankets.

She screamed and Maretta came running down the hall. In the next moment, she was scuttled from the room and the door was closed. She backed into the room facing her father's, it was empty and she sat on the floor, staring at her father's door. No one came out and no sound came from the room. She couldn't cry, couldn't think, couldn't move.

After what seemed like hours, Maretta finally came out and locked the door behind her, then rushed off down the stairs. She hadn't even looked at Natalie as she'd dashed off. Natalie pushed herself off the floor and strode to her father's door. They had no right to lock her out, away from him. She shook the knob, but it wouldn't open.

The house was silent. No matter how hard she listened, she could hear nothing. Natalie stilled her movements, waiting to hear if anyone would return. How could this happen? He'd been fine the day before. They had worked together, finishing everything he could help with, but now he would never help again. She rested her head against the cool door.

Papa.

He'd made her promise the night before and worked so hard to help her. Somehow, he'd known, he'd always known, that he wouldn't see the next day. He'd gotten her word so he could leave her. A tear finally broke free and it was as if it brought on a flood. The project was supposed to make her father want to stay, not allow him to go.

She ran down the hall back to her room and through her tears she collected all the pieces to Cody's leg, shoving them in a sack. She hefted it out to her father's wagon and ducked into the back. No one would miss her, not when they would have to worry about what to do with Father. Her brothers wouldn't need her, they never had. No one needed her anymore, now that Papa was gone. She sat in the silence for a moment, everything around her reminding her of the man who'd left. She couldn't stay there and look at his tools and plans, still tacked to the walls. She climbed up into the hay loft and hid in a back corner, crying herself to sleep.

THE CORNER WAS dark when she heard yelling. Someone was calling her name, but she couldn't tell who. Natalie's heart hurt too much to move, or yell that she was fine. She just wanted to be left all on her own. A small part of her never wanted to see anyone again.

Someone shuffled into the barn below her, searched around for something, then left without saying a word. Whoever was calling probably needed her for supper or something else unimportant. They didn't need her. Natalie closed her eyes again and curled into a ball. She'd had to be strong for months to help her father, but she could be weak now. She let the tears fall without wiping them. The hay scratched against her face and scalp, but mattered little.

Papa was with Mama now, and she wished she could be right along with them.

George yelled for her from somewhere nearby. He was angry. She could hear the gravel in his voice. He'd yelled like that any time she'd told Papa he'd done something against her wishes. George would yell and bluster about how she was Papa's favorite and Papa always listened to her. Maybe it had been true, but it wasn't anymore.

She wanted to yell down to him to go away, to let her be. She wanted to make everyone leave her be. If she could only find a place where no one could find her. She could stay there and hold onto her memories.

Natalie listened as closely as she could, but the yelling had stopped. She couldn't take a horse, but she *did* know the perfect place that was all alone. The ladder was difficult to see in the darkening shadows of the barn and she slid down the last few rungs. Outside, she scanned the area, but everyone had gone inside or at least out of sight. The whole ranch was eerily quiet as she strode through the yard.

The little house in the tree was in between the west and north pastures, where no one went. She could stay there and rest. Food didn't matter and neither did cold or damp, only getting somewhere people wouldn't yell for her or talk to her. She swiped at her eyes and made a run for the pasture, opened the gate, then ran as fast as she could toward the lonely little treehouse.

CHAPTER 26

Mr. Langerford stood near the entrance to his office and stared at Cody. Something about his look made the hair on the back of Cody's neck prickle. His boss rarely came out of his office unless he had an appointment and his niece had been in with him earlier.

As if on cue, Miss Greely ducked from behind her uncle and glanced all over the bank, finally finding him and setting a look of complete pity on him, the likes of which he hadn't seen in a long time. She took a deep breath and strode toward him, more like he was a guillotine than a man just sitting there. She stopped in front of the bars of his little nook.

"Yes, Miss Greely?" Her hard look of determination was sorely affected by the pure terror in her eyes.

"Mr. Hammond. I've been told to take you out to the Oleson Ranch immediately. Mr. Oleson has passed and, I'm afraid, there is some trouble in locating Miss Oleson. I don't know anything else. Anne sent this note to my uncle and he sent for me." She handed him a slip of paper.

He didn't bother to look at it, slipping it into his vest instead. "Miss Oleson is missing?" He took off his suit jacket during the day, preferring to work in his vest in the warm building. He shrugged back into it and slid his crutch under his arm, wasting no time.

"Hammond. Take whatever time you need." Mr. Langerford called as he let the barred door slam between the tellers and the common area of the bank.

"I'll send word back with Miss Greely." He slapped his hat on his head from the row of hooks in the back, then followed her out to the rig she'd used before.

"I'm sorry, Mr. Hammond. I don't know why he keeps asking me to drive you around when others are here to do it, but he insists." She refused to hold eye contact with him, making him wonder if that was the whole truth. Perhaps Mr. Langerford hoped that a match between Miss Greely and himself would keep the bank in the family. Cody chuckled as he shook his head, trying to think of what he could say that wouldn't embarrass her. "I'm sure he thinks I would be more comfortable with you, and he knows you are safe with me."

She waited until he was seated in the back, then climbed up to her spot and flicked the lines. She told him that, in the last week, she'd practiced and could now make them go where she intended. Her pretty blond hair was curled lightly and she sat with her back straight on the seat, but his mind noticed little else about her, as he focused on Natalie.

The Oleson Ranch was huge. It contained acre upon acre of pasture land with rolling hills and various buildings where they stored everything needed to run a ranch that size. Natalie could be anywhere. He finally slipped the paper from his pocket and skimmed it. Natalie had been missing for one whole day. They had expected her to come home the previous evening, but she hadn't returned.

He didn't know the ranch well, only what he could see as they drove by on the way to the house and what he'd been told. He didn't have the ability to go out into the pastures, nor had he ever had the desire. That left him at a disadvantage. Was there anywhere someone could hide that was beyond the buildings by the barn? Only the Oleson boys would know.

Miss Greely seemed unwilling to make the horses go any faster than a walk and after an hour, she slumped a little in the seat. "Are we nearing the ranch? I didn't expect it to be so far." She drew her little kerchief from her bag and dabbed at her forehead.

"You've got another few miles to go. Might want to make those horses work a little harder, or it will be dark before we get there. As it is, you'll have to drive home at least part of the way in the dark."

She gasped and pulled the lines closer to her, making the horses stop completely. "But, what about bears?"

He laughed slightly and saw her bristle at the sound. "No need to worry about a bear, but maybe a few coyotes. They won't hurt you, though."

She flicked the lines hard and the horses jumped into motion. They finally reached the ranch and after he struggled his way out, she called to him. "Mr. Hammond? Do you think you could have someone drive me home?" Her voice was a squeak.

John Oleson stood from where he sat on the front step. He was tall and lanky and Cody had almost mistaken him for his cousin Eli. "Let me get my horse.

I'll drive you back in, miss." He touched his hat, then passed Cody on the way to the barn.

"You'll be all right out here, then, or do you want to come in and wait?" Cody turned back to her to make sure she was fine.

"You go on inside. I don't know if they've brought out Mr. Oleson yet and I don't like to be in the same house as someone who's dead. I just—" She shivered instead of continuing.

"Dying is just another step. You can't escape it. Thank you for the ride and I hope John takes good care of you on the way back." He touched his hat and went inside. If it had been George offering, he'd have advised her to decline, but he had no reason to think John would be the same.

Most of the family sat around the huge dinner table, minus his sister Anne and John. "Where is Anne? I would think you would've sent her to come for me." He tugged off his hat and found an empty chair around the table.

Nathan answered, "Anne acts as the undertaker, so she has been busy and couldn't bring you out, though she told us she would send you a note today."

He slipped it from his pocket and held it up. "What do we know and where have you looked?" He searched the table. One set of Oleson boys looked somber, their younger cousins brooded in angry silence. George finally broke it.

"We've checked everywhere around this ranch. She was always trying to be the center of attention, hated it when we wouldn't listen to her and her bossing. She tried to be Ma all this time, but she isn't and won't ever be."

"Not now, George." Charles wacked him in the arm.

Nathan had a map of the ranch spread out on the

table and Cody ignored the brothers. They were dealing with the loss of their father and the disappearance of their sister. Their anger was understandable. There were red marks on the map and Nathan pointed to each one.

"These are all areas where we thought she might be. Barton was sure she would be in the old treehouse, but he checked there right away and it was empty. We've checked all the machine sheds and as much of the pastures as we can. There's a lot of ground to cover."

He stared at the map, working out where it might be likely for her to go. "Did you check in her wagon?" It seemed easy, but often people missed the obvious.

"Yes, we're sure she was there at some point, because there's a bag there that John said was not there a week ago." Nathan pointed to the building where the wagon was stored.

"How well does she know the ranch?" Cody asked. She'd only been there for two weeks and most of that she'd spent with her father. She couldn't have known much.

"Barton took her around to show her, but she was in a hurry," Nathan said. "We're mostly worried at this point that she wandered off, thinking she knew where she was going, and got lost."

Cody's whole body went cold. "Are you saying she could've spent the night outside in the pasture?"

Nathan sat back down in his chair and stared at the map. "That's exactly what I'm saying."

CHAPTER 27

Summer heat had kept her warm all through the evening in the little house in the tree, but she'd shivered all through the night. The day had been lost to the sleep she couldn't manage all night. Natalie's belly ached with hunger after going so long without food. Part of her didn't want to go on, didn't want to be alone in the world, but she knew she had to leave her spot and go back.

Her stomach rumbled loudly and she curled into a ball, clutching her knees to her chest. She'd been in just that position after Papa told her Mama had not made it through the night. She could remember brief moments from the following weeks, just images. Calling forth the emotion would make her cry all over again.

Cody had challenged her with his words and she'd said, without much thought at all, that those that passed were probably happier, better off, so why couldn't she let Mama go? If it was true, that Mama was happier, then it was selfish to still mourn so deeply after ten years. She forced her clenched fist to relax, and release. Forced her lungs to breathe in, and out. All releases. All good for her.

Natalie closed her eyes as the tears flowed. It was time to release what she'd been holding onto, because she couldn't even mourn her Papa, until she made peace with Mama's death.

I love you…I miss you…But, I've got to let you go.

The heaviness that held her down released. While her heart still ached for her father, she'd gotten to see him, spend time with him. He'd told her what he expected of her and even given her his blessing for her future. She would miss him dearly, but it was time to face what she'd run from.

She had to eat, and face her brothers. She had to face the family she'd left to deal with her father, and she needed comfort from the one man who wouldn't give it—Cody.

Her father had, in his own way, given her his blessing with Cody. If a man could know down to the day when he would pass, if he could raise her and love her, couldn't he also choose the man who was best for her? Even though he hadn't met Cody, was it possible he knew? She'd been drawn to him since arriving in Belle Fourche and his change of heart over the last few days had made him even more desirable. But would he take her? Would he want a woman to clutter up his ordered life?

He was a man of meticulous decisions and she was a woman who tended to be impetuous as her father had said. Would they grate upon each other, or temper their faults? Natalie opened the inner shutter of the window facing east. She could just make out the house and the barn in the distance, but no movement. It was too far away. She had a long walk before she made it back and probably even longer to explain her absence before she could eat. Best to get it done with. Worst of all, she couldn't have explained at the time why she'd run in the first place. She'd just needed time alone, to think.

She trudged in the direction of the house, letting the scent of the clover on the breeze fill her nose. Now that she was on the ground, she couldn't see the house or much of anything beyond the next hill. Some of the land in Belle Fourche was flat as you please, but the Oleson land rolled, as if it wanted to be part of the mountains, but just wasn't quite close enough. As she neared the house, she heard people talking and horses whickering. Charles turned to search the horizon and caught sight of her. He stood higher in his saddle and she waved to him, too tired to do more.

He turned his horse toward her and kicked it to a run, reaching her quickly. He reached down to her and when she looked up into his face, she couldn't miss the concern.

"Where have you been? We've all been so worried." He tugged her easily into the saddle in front of him and she rested against her brother. Though he was younger, he hadn't been smaller than her for a long time and she let him be strong where she couldn't.

"I had to think, away from people." She was too tired to fight with him.

"They've taken him to town to ready his body for burial. You weren't here to tell us what to do."

She closed her eyes, but his words bit her hard in the chest. "I'm sorry. I've spent the last ten years trying to fill the spot Mama left. I was no good at it. I'm sure you will all resent me for the rest of your days, but it's how I dealt with losing her. I thought, maybe, if I stepped into her place, you all might not miss her so much. Maybe you wouldn't have to go through what I was dealing with." She sobbed and covered her face. Charles reached around her and held her tight.

"We did for a long time. George still does, because he holds onto everything, but as we got older, we understood."

"Did you?" She hadn't figured out until she'd been alone to really think about her mother and father and how she would go on, exactly what she'd done to her brothers to turn them against her. "Because I didn't. I didn't see it. It's like I started without realizing why."

"You were only eighteen. Still young. Pa was too heartsick to tell you to stop, so he told us to ignore you instead of getting angry. Trouble was, he was too heartsick to really be a pa to us, so you were all we had."

"I'm so sorry, Charles." She leaned into his strength, glad to finally have a connection to one of her brothers.

"I am too. Pa's advice was usually pretty sound, but not right after Ma died, and he never really corrected himself after."

"He should've just told me to hush." She wiped her eyes and Chales sighed.

"He couldn't. He loved you too much and you looked too much like Ma for him to ever say anything against you."

"I don't know what I'll do without him. He made me promise to stop making limbs. I'll be all alone. I'm not a man, so I won't get a share of Oleson land." Though she didn't want it to, the fear made her voice pitch higher until she clamped her mouth shut.

"Nathan and Maretta won't send you away. Not to mention, there's one angry man waiting for you in their dining room."

"Angry?" He could only mean Cody. Though he

never yelled, he always managed to look like he might at any moment.

"Mr. Hammond was furious that no one kept an eye on you after you found Pa. Especially with how close you were to him. He's put down pages of notes and a plan to find you. He'll be mighty glad you're back safely."

As they drew close to the crowd of horsemen waiting for them, Charles pulled his horse to a stop and dismounted, then helped her down. George was off his horse in an instant and had a hold of her arms. He gave her one harsh shake.

"What were you thinking, running off like that? Didn't you think we'd be worried? Didn't you think we'd need to deal with arrangements for Pa instead of trying to find you? Can't you ever just stop and think?"

Barton was to George before he could even finish and yanked his cousin away. "Stop. She didn't mean to do anything. Just leave her be."

George grabbed the reins of his horse and stormed off toward the barn. The other men in the circle remained silent and Natalie rubbed her arms where her brother had gripped her. It hadn't been hard—his words had hit her harder than his touch. Now that her eyes were clear, she could see just what she'd done, and he had every right to be angry.

Natalie slowly made her way up the front porch steps, then pushed into the house. She could hear Cody talking, even from the other end of the house. She followed his voice back to the dining room and opened the door. He sat on the other side of the table, his hair rumpled where he'd run his hands through it. His eyes were narrow and he stared at the paper until he felt her presence and looked up.

The moment he saw her, he stood, using the table to brace himself. "Natalie…"

She came around the table and before she could ask for forgiveness for scaring him and making him come all the way out there, he pulled her to his chest and held her close in a tight embrace. He balanced his hip against the table, then she felt both arms surround her, hold her, comfort her.

"I haven't been that worried in a long time. Where have you been?" He ran his hands through her snarled hair.

"It doesn't matter," she mumbled. "I've had time to think. I'm sorry I needed it, but everything is clearer now." Her stomach rumbled, reminding her she hadn't eaten.

Maretta stood from the other end of the table and frowned. "You can't have eaten in a whole day. You two sit for a moment while I go get some leftover ham from last night."

Natalie waited for Cody to sit, but as soon as she was seated next to him, he took her hand in his. Perhaps Papa was right, Cody would be the man to take his place. Not to be a father to her, as she joked, but to look after her and care for her.

Cody's eyes sought hers. "I'm so glad you're home. Please, next time you feel like running…run to me."

CHAPTER 28

Though he'd certainly noticed that she was pretty, Cody had never really allowed himself the luxury of investigating every line of Natalie's face and form. Just as the drawing had become more real the more lines he added, the more she came into focus when he took account of her so close to him.

She sat quietly, eating the meal Maretta had brought in and left for her. They were alone in the dining room, but since the room was so large and open, he felt more on display than private. Without thinking, he grabbed his crutch and stood, giving Natalie a moment to eat in peace. He had so many questions that only she could answer.

He'd never been drawn to one person so completely and to love something was to know it, completely, until it wasn't a surprise anymore. Yet, every time he encountered her, he couldn't predict what would happen. She was new every moment, yet still the same woman. He strode over to a painting, needing to stay near her, yet wanting to give her time.

He'd barely noticed the painting before she appeared at his side and rested her forehead against his shoulder. His heart tripped over itself that she was so willing to reach for him when he'd been such a brute to her. "I'm sorry, Natalie. I think I said it before, but I can never apologize enough. You should've just turned and fled from me instead of staying the course and proving me for the unworthy dog I am."

She slipped his arm around her waist and wrapped her arms carefully around him. "And if I had done that, you would still be just the same, and so would I. If I had run away, today would be much harder than it is."

He took in a deep breath and closed his eyes, allowing himself to feel to his very depths what it was like for a woman to care. If anyone had in the past, he couldn't remember it. He'd gone from spoiled and wealthy, part of a cold family who felt little for anyone outside of themselves, to a poor invalid, cast off to the dregs of society. Nowhere along that path had he found anyone except for his own sister—and only briefly—who cared about him outside of what he could do for them. Natalie didn't even know what he could do for her. She'd only been interested in what she could provide for him. He'd truly never met anyone like her.

"I'm sorry too, Cody. I'm sorry that in my utter sadness I didn't think of you first. You were far away and my focus wouldn't expand beyond the house, the ranch, in fact, beyond the moment I was in. I could think of no one but myself and my father."

He turned so that she didn't embrace him from the side, but directly in front of him. No matter that it was more difficult for him with his crutch, he wanted to hold her, to comfort her. If only he'd been there for her, right there at the ranch, when she'd needed him.

"I gave you no reason to believe you could count on me. But that will change." When had comforting someone become easy? When had he learned what to say and how to return that slight smile to her face? Was that only because he wanted to know her more than any other, or had he been made specifically to fill that need, and so had been woefully inadequate to everyone else until he'd met her? It was yet another problem to take to his notebook, and one he relished thinking more about.

She stood so serenely next to him, her eyes sweet and wide. "I've always been adaptable, on the move. Though, I would like to stay here now. It would be nice to grow roots instead of pretending I'm a feather on the breeze."

And just like that, his last wisp of desire to return to England died. If Natalie was here, there would be no leaving. The last hint of anger toward Anne for staying to marry Eli died as well and a soft contentment blanketed his heart. "Then stay you will, and I will stay right here with you. From now on, you can rely on me. I will be as unchanging as a rock."

She tipped her face to look at him and her soft eyes implored him. His heart tripped and his arm stiffened, pulling her closer. He'd never had the opportunity, or the desire, to kiss a woman, but the moment was suddenly ripe with opportunity.

Natalie's eyes widened slightly and her lips parted as if she were going to speak, but she said nothing. He'd never been shy, nor particularly hesitant, but Natalie had just lost her father and he didn't want to take advantage. Yet it felt so right to have her there, just then, and the only way to bring her even closer was to complete what his heart desired.

He wet his suddenly dry lips and she glanced to watch the action, lighting the flame in him further. He leaned down and met her lips, softer than down, much softer than he expected. Could nothing about this woman ever be predictable?

She burst away from him, her eyes wide and a tear coursed down her cheek. "I—" Her tongue darted out and licked her own lips. "I don't think I'm ready for this yet."

With but a moment for him to catch his unbalanced weight back on his cane, she ran from the room.

CHAPTER 29

It took two days to make all the arrangements for Papa, but in that time Natalie worked without stopping on Cody's new leg. She relinquished all the control that had been so important and let her brothers and her aunt and uncle handle everything while she immersed herself in the last little bit of her father's life she would have, the trade she'd agreed to give up.

Somewhere in the late nights and the hot days she realized Cody had not returned to see her. She'd run out on him after his kiss and probably embarrassed him. She'd certainly embarrassed herself. It had been so unexpected. She'd been staring into his eyes, they were so different from anyone else's, a gray that didn't take on a blue no matter how hard she looked. Then, he'd just kissed her and it had been such a shock she hadn't known what to do.

Now that she'd had a few days to think on it, her mind tried to prod her into forgetting it but it just wasn't possible. She'd hoped he would return and explain to her what had happened. What did it mean? Did he intend to see her again, or just avoid her? And was it too soon to expect any of that? Then, between all the confusing thoughts of Cody, would come the heavy thoughts of losing Papa.

With the shaping of the leg, each step reminded her of what her father would've done. She remembered what he'd said about her design and she doubted every move. Would Cody tell her if it was uncomfortable? Would the disappointment remind her of Papa?

John appeared at the door of the old wagon and he watched her for a moment.

"Seems strange. The wagon without Pa. It's just not the same," he mumbled.

She'd felt the same way when she'd come out to try to finish what she'd started and it still lingered.

"After I'm finished, we should decide if we will sell it or just clean it out," she said.

"You're really going to listen to what he said. I'm surprised." He spread his feet wide and crossed his arms.

"He didn't just say it. I gave my word. This will be the last one. I wouldn't even keep doing this except I got the feeling he wanted me to finish this one. He never met Cody, but he talked about him. I think he would want to see this done."

"Would he, or would you?"

She stopped and laid the leather she was working with aside. "Both, I think. Father seemed to think that Cody would be the one for me. I need to decide if I will stay and explore that further or leave and continue on."

"How would you survive? George and Charles have already said they are staying here with me. We are happy here. There's nothing for you outside of Belle Fourche besides pain."

The tears came so easy the last few days and John's

words brought on another wave. "What if I stay and realize Papa was wrong? What if I stay and Cody doesn't want me? He seems like the best option. I think about him so often, but I'm hurting so much right now. How can I make a choice like that?"

John kicked the dirt then shifted his hat. "I don't see that you have to decide right now. Nathan and Maretta are happy to have you stay. I don't even know if they would approve of you leaving, though you're old enough to have a mind of your own. Just remember, it's not good to make a decision like that when you're torn up inside. Maretta sent me out here to tell you the service starts in two hours. We need to leave in one."

Natalie glanced down at her dress, stained with varnish and dirty with wear. She'd never had to dress up for Papa before, but she had to now. It would be expected of her to look her best, even if her face was puffy from tears.

Two hours later, she sat in the front of the church waiting for the service to start. A few townspeople came simply because they liked the Olesons. Some came out of curiosity, and still others came because of the offer of a free lunch following.

Cody arrived along with his boss and Miss Greely. He glanced at her, but held back, letting his gaze wander all around the room. Her stomach pitched and she held her breath, waiting for him to come over to see her. After two days, he had to miss her, but a funeral was the wrong place to discuss what had happened in the dining room at the ranch.

She moved to the Oleson pew and took her seat. All around her, the voices of Aunt Maretta and all her brothers, the cousins and their wives lingered around. None of them, not even her brothers, knew Papa like she did. They hadn't worked with him. They hadn't listened to his stories. They would all go on and just be who they'd always been, but part of her would be missing.

"May I sit next to you?" Miss Greely wore a dark gray dress with a fashionable ruffled front. Natalie hadn't owned a black dress at all and had to wear a dark blue.

Natalie motioned for her to sit, but didn't trust her voice. Not with her father laying in the pine box in the front of the church. She hadn't seen him since that morning three days before and the sight choked her.

"I'm so sorry for your loss." She handed Natalie a soft embroidered kerchief.

Natalie accepted it, but still didn't speak. Others seemed able to without any issue but her own throat felt lodged, almost shut.

"I'm Alicia, by the way. I don't know a soul here in Belle Fourche other than your brother and Mr. Hammond minimally. I usually can't even bear to talk to anyone." She flushed deeply. "Do listen to me prattle on like a ninny." She clutched her hands in her lap, bowing her head.

Natalie nodded, avoiding pointing out the fact that she'd just introduced herself to a relative stranger. The only reason she knew who Miss Greely was came from her brother, who had told her all about the young woman.

Once the dam was opened, Miss Greely seemed to talk freely. "I really do think I'm a lost cause. It is my uncle's hope that I will attract the attention of one particular eligible man and secure the bank for the future, since my uncle has no children."

She chattered on with a similar expression and speed of a student who freshly learned their spelling words and had to tell them before forgetting once again. Natalie glanced at Alicia for a moment and she smiled back, a warm and genuine smile.

Natalie cleared her throat to engage the woman who'd decided to be her friend. "Belle Fourche is pretty full of cowboys. How does your uncle expect to find one that will want to take over the bank?"

"Oh, that's simple. He's already chosen one for me—Cody Hammond."

CHAPTER 30

Two days after the funeral, Cody finally heard from Natalie. He'd wanted to talk to her after the service, but she'd been surrounded by her family or Miss Greely the entire time she'd been there. He'd watched her with great care, but she hadn't looked for him.

He'd wanted to send her out a note with Anne, but that wouldn't be private either and he didn't know how to ask her what he wanted to. How did one ask if she hated him after he'd kissed her? He couldn't put that into a note. The very thought left him nervous. Her brothers would probably chase him right off the property. If her response to his kiss predicted her own feelings, *she* might run him off.

The note she'd sent held no clue either. Once again, she was a mystery. He'd tried writing down his notes about what had happened and what might happen and then he'd tossed them all in the fire, knowing she would do something completely different anyway. Even the fact that she'd sent a note was unexpected. He'd been hoping she missed him and would come in herself.

After work, he rode out to the ranch with Anne. She was tired and had little to say. It was almost like it had been before, where he would've kept her silent with his brooding.

"Has Natalie mentioned anything to you?" He glanced at Anne as she drove.

"I don't see her often. She caught me as I was leaving this morning."

He waited a moment, hopeful Anne would continue talking. He needed chatter or something to fill up his mind because he wasn't sure what a fitting of his new leg might be like. He wasn't squeamish about many things, but showing Natalie the bumpy, misshapen appendage, made him nervous. Talking to her after their last encounter only heightened it until he wanted to just pitch himself off the wagon as an excuse to get out of the next few hours.

"Will you want to stay tonight, or should I talk to Eli about bringing you back in?" Anne flicked the lines, either completely unaware of his predicament or thankful for a way to make him squirm for a change.

"I'm not certain. If Natalie would rather I not stay, then I will need to go back to town."

"Why would she have you leave? You haven't had a chance to sit with her in days."

He was glad of the chance to talk, but he hadn't wanted to talk about her. It only made him clutch the seat even harder. "I may have done something that bothered her."

"That's not surprising. You often do." She raised an eyebrow, but kept facing forward.

"Is that all you have to say? I may have destroyed the

one good thing in my life and all you can do is throw a retort at me?"

"Wait." Anne let the lines loosen and the horses slowed their pace. "Are you telling me you and Natalie —?" She sucked in her upper lip. "But Mr. Langerford has been telling everyone that you and Miss Greely will soon be together."

He shook his head and prayed his boss hadn't done even more damage than he'd done himself. "No, not Alicia. Will you be there when she tries the prosthesis?" The subject matter couldn't stay on Natalie or Anne might press him for more details on his feelings, details he couldn't answer until he was sure he hadn't ruined everything.

"Yes, she was quite nervous about doing it alone. Especially since it involves you undressing a bit." She gave him a sly look and laughed at whatever expression he made.

"Don't worry, Cody. I'm sure there will be plenty of time for you to prepare once we get there."

He hung his head. The woman would run away from him now for sure.

NATALIE WAITED in the sunroom with the leg, pacing from one end of the hot room to the other. Ever since she'd talked to Alicia Greely at her father's funeral, she'd tried to get a handle on her growing feelings for Cody. If he was going to be paired with someone else, especially someone who could further his career and was incredibly beautiful, she wouldn't stand in his way. Even if he had kissed her first.

Her heart screamed at her, that he had held her, and

had kissed her, and had made her think about him for days. But he hadn't come to talk to her at the funeral, and he hadn't come out to the ranch since. She'd wanted him to come on his own to see her, to check on her, but instead of waiting for him, she'd sent him a note the moment she was finished with his new leg.

She heard the wagon pull up to the front of the house and felt her whole body tremble. Should she go to the door and let him in, or let Maretta do it so that she wouldn't dissolve in front of everyone? Her knees went weak and she heard the slow, rhythmic movements of his crutch along with soft talking as he, Maretta, and Anne made their way down the hall.

They pushed through the door and the moment his eyes caught hers, she clutched the table for support. Maretta left them and Anne helped Cody get comfortable in a chair, then seated herself nearby.

"This is fascinating to me. We amputated limbs in the hospital in London, but I've never gotten to see anyone replace them." Anne smiled as she glanced between Natalie and Cody. "Where should we start?"

Cody turned a little red around the ears and Natalie wanted to reassure him, but until he tried the leg on, she couldn't say that it would be fine. It might bother him or not fit. Then she would have to try to adjust it.

"Unfortunately, with all the straps to keep it attached, you will have to undress down to your long johns." She felt heat suffuse her face, even though she'd been there many times to help her father with this step and had assisted him to get the fit correct, it had never bothered her until now, when she had to help a man she knew better than all of them put together.

Anne stood and laid a hand on her shoulder. "Why

don't you go get us something cool to drink? I'll help Cody get ready."

She nodded and left the room, taking her time while she gathered everything, and more still on the way back so she didn't spill. Once she returned, Cody sat in the same chair in a one-piece cotton undergarment. It completely covered him, but he shifted in his seat and crossed his arms. He wouldn't look her directly in the eyes.

Natalie set down the tray with drinks, but instead of pouring anything, she went right to gathering the leg and all the straps. Once he had it on, he could get dressed again and they would both be comfortable. She adjusted it over his thigh and told him where each strap had to go so that he could maneuver easier and not have it flop around, or worse, fall off. He used the table to help him, but as soon as it was secured, he stood and the leg held him.

He attempted a few steps with Anne's help, but it was still too new for him to take much of a walk.

"I'll see if I can get a cane for you to use while you get sure on your feet again." Anne helped him back into his clothes, then he sat down. Sweat trickled down his face and Natalie grabbed a napkin to wipe it for him. He met her eyes and Anne laughed.

"I think it's time I let you two talk alone. I'll be out here with Maretta. The door is open."

Natalie didn't watch her leave or say goodbye, she was too enchanted by Cody's eyes.

"What are you thinking about?" he asked her, reaching for her hand.

"I don't know what I'm thinking, but even worse, I don't know what you're thinking." She was so confused.

Her heart wanted to be with him, but not if he wasn't going to stay with her.

"Oh, I was thinking that it's been too long since I've seen you."

"I was giving you time. I didn't know what to feel and then I was told you were to be paired with Alicia." Just saying it hurt her heart.

"Miss Greely? I have no such plans." He chuckled softly and touched her cheek. His hands were cool against her hot skin.

"I was so worried I'd offended you or hurt you." She searched his face for the truth because he was the most expressive man she'd ever met.

"Not at all. I didn't ask your leave before I kissed you. It was completely my fault." He smiled for a moment then leaned forward, his voice little more than a whisper, "May I have leave to kiss you again?"

Her heart leapt and she couldn't breathe. She'd wanted that most of all. Natalie leaned forward with a breathless, "Yes."

He took his time, caressed her cheek for a moment and tucked little wisps of hair behind her ears, then he leaned forward and led her face to his. She knew what to do this time, if not completely what to expect. He gently swept her up in his kiss until it felt as if her feet no longer touched the floor, her body suspended, her heart bursting, and life would never be the same again.

CHAPTER 31

All the family had told them to wait, and for once Natalie agreed to avoid impetuousness. They spent every evening talking and planning Cody's house and their future. Cody purchased a small plot of land just outside of Belle Fourche for the both of them. All the Olesons helped build the house and, after only a few weeks, it was nearly completed.

The August heat bore down on Natalie as she walked to the church alongside Alicia. Though there had been a misunderstanding, it hadn't stopped them from becoming friends. Alicia had never truly desired Cody. Natalie understood now that it was Alicia's uncle who had desired the match. Mr. Langerford wasn't pleased that he would have to find someone else for his niece, but he did seem happy that Cody would no longer be alone.

Everyone was shocked when Cody started walking without use of any crutches or cane. He'd always been strong, he'd just needed a reason to build his strength back up. Walking with Natalie in the evenings had been enough of a goal that he'd worked hard and had accomplished it.

Alicia took Natalie aside in the church as they waited for everyone to arrive and get seated. She was nervous as other members sat all around them. Every time she sat in the church, she remembered her father and she prayed her wedding would eventually dispel that sadness. John came in, followed by George and Charles. He tipped his hat to her, then stopped for a moment and swaggered over.

Natalie heard Alicia's gasp as her brother joined them. "You look right pretty, Natalie. You do, too, Miss Alicia." He nodded and she noted that though he'd complimented her first, his eyes never left the pretty blonde.

"Alicia needs someone to sit with, John. Would you like to?" She almost laughed at the confusion on her poor brother's face.

"Sit? Isn't she sitting with you?"

"Yes, but this place will be needed when the rest of the family comes. Her uncle is not here today, she'll be all alone over in his spot," Natalie explained. But her brother just scratched his chin, still not looking at her. "Hold out your elbow, John," she whispered.

Her friend turned pink. "Are you sure you want to?" she whispered.

A smile broke over his whole face. "Yes, I think I would." He offered his arm and she glanced at Natalie for a moment, then took it.

Cody's hitched walk made him easy to spot as he walked into the church and sat in the spot Alicia had just left. He took her hand. "I wonder how long we should wait to tell them we don't want to have a big service?"

If her father hadn't given his approval the very night

before he passed, her decision may have been different, but he'd given his blessing and she was too mature to wait. "I'm ready whenever you are. I would ask Pastor O'Hare to do it right after the service today if we were ready."

He took her hand and squeezed it. "We'll be ready soon enough. And when it's time, nothing will get in our way."

ALSO BY KARI TRUMBO

Don't miss book Five in the Brothers of Belle Fourche series

Made in the USA
Columbia, SC
31 August 2019